A SCIENTIFIC LOOK
AT THE CONCEPT OF SOUL

An Attempted Synthesis

A SCIENTIFIC LOOK AT THE CONCEPT OF SOUL
An Attempted Synthesis

Anil Vishnu Moharir

ZORBA BOOKS

ZORBA BOOKS

Published in India by Zorba Books, 2017

Website: www.zorbabooks.com
Email: info@zorbabooks.com

ISBN Print Book - 978-93- 5265-930-2

Zorba Books Pvt. Ltd.(opc)
Gurugram, INDIA

Printed at : Repro Knowledgecast Limited, Thane

Dear Anil,

Yes I have looked through your recent article. It's very dense with a lot of material, some of it decidedly controversial, such as your view of Christian history in relation to reincarnation.

Here in Britain religious dogma is not a major problem. Only about 7% of the population have any regular religious activity. The great majority are utterly ignorant of religious traditions and haven't the faintest idea of what the word soul might mean. Your overview ties together many different strands of thought with modern physiology and points to deeper interconnections within physics.

There is so much in your article that it's impossible to comment in detail on it, and indeed to read it with the thoroughness it deserves would take a long time. I'm sorry I simply haven't had time to devote this amount of attention.

Best wishes
Rupert Sheldrake
Ph.D. Cambridge; Frank Knox
Fellow-Harvard University, British Researcher,
Author and Critic

CONTENTS

FOREWORD

Ever since Georges Lemaitre (1894–1966), Belgian astronomer and cosmologist, observed that all heavenly bodies (stars and galaxies) are moving away from each other at a very high speed, inferring thereby that the universe probably had its origin in a cataclysmic explosion of a small primeval 'body', all recent experimental evidence has been pointing in the same direction. This observation now goes by the popular term 'the big bang', first proposed somewhat derisively by the British astronomer and astrophysicist Sir Fred Hoyle, the proponent of the 'steady state theory of universe'. This theory holds that our universe did not get created, but is pristine and has always existed as it is. This work was done together with Jayant Narlikar, an Indian astrophysicist. The changes within this universe may appear to be evolutionary in nature, yet can be explained by the existing laws of physics. The Jains or the followers of Jainism in India also hold a similar point of view. Gautama Buddha seemed to have been reluctant to speculate as to how our universe could have come about, and instead advised his followers to focus on the infirmities of this sensorial world. The Middle Eastern Abrahamic religions are too theistic to be included in this kind of discussion.

It is in one of the other branches of Indian philosophy traditionally associated with Hinduism that we find references to theories on the origin of the universe. These speculations are diverse, but each one of them takes for granted that the universe had a beginning from a single source. One such speculation states in a verse, 'With heat the Brahma expands and what follows are matter, life, mind and man'. It also calls this progressively changing scenario as 'karma'. The word 'Brahma' given to this primal body implies a process

1

of expansion because it comes from the Sanskrit root *Brih*, meaning to spread or to roar. The modern theories in astronomical/cosmological physics or cosmogenesis appear to have a similar viewpoint in which the thing that expanded is called a singularity, because nothing else existed at that time (which has been calculated to be about 14 billion years ago). Even in theoretical physics, the nature of this singular entity is admitted to be beyond comprehension, at least in the foreseeable future. Language fails here because in the absence of space, no movement is possible; therefore, a verb cannot be used; since it is single, comparisons are not feasible and, hence, adjectives cannot be used either; and to give it a name becomes superfluous. 'That thing', if it can be called as such, is speculated to be in a state of utter or absolute equivalence in terms of forces, if any, within it. How and why this equivalence gets to be tweaked leading to the events that follow is likely to remain a mystery in the foreseeable future, but the nature of the violent and extremely hot events that followed this change are now somewhat within the grasp of human understanding.

As the details get worked out, one thing must remain uncontested that the singularity or Brahma is our forbearer. 'Forefather' would be a wrong word because the evolution of gender is a very recent event in comparison to the estimated time of 14 billion years ago, when the singularity or Brahma exploded, and subsequently began to expand. In what is probably an all-time classic, Sant Dnyaneshwar (AD 1275–96), a philosopher extraordinaire from Maharashtra, while narrating a commentary on *Shrimad Bhagavadgita* in his very first verse, uses the word *atmaroopa* to describe this basic singularity. The word is in two parts—*atma* meaning force and *roopa* implying form. This is as good a definition or description of the singularity as you can get, because it encapsulates the sequence of events that followed the 'big bang'. The forms that are inherited from this singularity must carry in them the forces that occupied the singularity till they last or speculatively get rolled back into the singularity after the original force that caused the expansion wanes and when gravitational forces take over and the universe collapses or rolls back on itself, as happens to many a star during their lifetime in this universe.

At a fundamental level, what we call as the inanimate universe ticks on due to a play of energy and it is this energy that, at some point, comes to express itself as living matter, albeit only in a few molecules, but this transformation has enormous implications. As living matter develops and becomes more complex, the energy or force within the living cells evolves into a more sophisticated form and performs an array of functions. Modern physics, beginning with Einstein, have described matter and energy as two faces of the same coin in that in an atom, its constituents such as electrons manifest and disappear leaving behind a trail, which can only be experienced post facto, and then regenerate again as a particle.

This trail is viewed as electrical in nature for want of a better word. In living organisms, where a complicated array of atoms, molecules, and compounds work in tandem during life, the routes that get established to keep the systems going are called 'ion channels', for it is the ionic form of the atom which is responsible for the end use and the consequent result. This extraordinary play is possible because it is codified in the genome, which virtually acts as a choreographer to sustain life. The genome is vulnerable to change by atmospheric radiation, sensitive as it is, and though it may undergo a change, it continues to sustain itself as a reproductive unit ushering in changes both in function and structure in its new 'avatar'. The word avatar, meaning incarnation or reincarnation, hints subtly that the same clay which, in fact, is in a 'modified energy state' is now manifesting in a different form.

The word 'maya' frequently used by Indian philosophers needs to be explained here. This, in fact, means the creative potential of Brahma or the singularity. The observable universe or the nature at large, as we see it, is a part of this creative impulse and, according to some philosophers, is as real as the singularity; on the other hand, some philosophers believe that only Brahma is the absolute truth relegating the manifested world to a somewhat inferior position, calling it a 'relative truth'.

Dr Anil Moharir, a physicist with vast experience in agricultural research, was in a unique position to observe nature in all its splendour, but notably he did not stop at the feeling of wonder. He has not only delved deep into the literature on the subject of botany and plantology (plant-biology), but has also made researches in physics which, by a common agreement, is now considered to be the fountainhead of all matters scientific. He therefore goes back across huge swathes of time to espouse the idea of unity (the soul) of this variegated universe and, yet, allows within his arguments, the 'energy-based mechanization' of both the non-living as well as the living matter. In the mind of this reviewer, Dr Moharir might be introducing an entirely new branch of philosophy to the existing schools. In this small book, Dr Moharir has proposed four new premises and has logically discussed them in the light of modern theories and with the help of Standard Model of Elementary Particle Physics. They are:

(a) The hitherto enigmatic 'soul' is nothing else but the *de facto primal* electric charge.

(b) Souls of all living organisms remain in continual connection from their birth to death with universal electric energy continuum or cosmic consciousness.

(c) Rebirth/reincarnation of individual souls is scientifically impossible and continues to be a popular myth rather than a scientific truth.

(d) Rebirth/reincarnation merely represents the birth of a new individual, resembling in its characteristics with someone who had lived in the historical past arising out of the self-replicating behaviour of the deoxyribonucleic acid (DNA) molecules in associated interaction with epigenetic environment which, in fact, is a modified version of the original electrical environment.

The technical terminology that he employs is erudite, yet is well within the scope of an average reader with a modicum of scientific background, such as this reviewer and the way he marshals his facts is 'awesome', to use a popular modern expression. His view, stretching the Indian intellectual tradition to nearly 10,000 years ago, appeared to me far-fetched during the first reading of his book, but recent researches since then have unearthed data which suggests that Dr Moharir might be justified in his conclusions in this regard.

To sum up, this book is a *tour de force* and those who read it are sure to have an enriching experience. I congratulate Dr Anil Moharir on this painstaking task and showing enough courage to back his scientific intuition and also for presenting a holistic multidisciplinary overview of the complex and socioculturally controversial subjects of 'soul' and 'rebirth'. This is a splendid effort. For me, it had been a great pleasure and also a rewarding experience to read this book.

46, Shirish Co-Op. Hsg. Society   **Ravin Thatte**
187, Veer Savarkar Marg,
Mumbai, Maharashtra 400 016

PREFACE

The concepts of 'soul' and 'rebirth' have been associated with human psyche for millions of years and have become a part and parcel of our religious dogmatic faith. Throughout history, all cultures have postulated the existence of soul. Psychology, the scientific field of discipline, is supposed to study everything about soul. Even so, psychologists in practise do not actually study soul, but only human behaviour and, more recently, the human brain. Still, a substantial majority of the human population across the world does not subscribe to the concept of soul for various reasons. They also do not have logical reasons for explaining the continued existence and repeated emergence of the characteristics, features, and traits of all the living species on earth in cycles of birth and death. Despite millions of years that have gone by in the history of existence on earth, man is still searching for his roots of origin and the force that drives him from birth to death. This book traces the developments in the efforts and difficulties encountered in understanding the enigmatic concepts of soul and rebirth that have been discussed for over 10,000 years and, yet, being far away from a global consensus. The reasons are more of religious dogma, pride, divide, blind faith, false sense of superiority of one religion over other and, above all, fear and lack of courage on the part of people to cross the religious and social barriers arising out of the teachings, interpretations, beliefs, and dogma of religious and metanarrative books to rebel in favour of purely scientific logic, reason, and truth. Both the concepts of soul and rebirth have been propagated and entrenched in the minds of people for thousands of years, more by the religious preachers as part of their philosophies than on scientific merits. Not surprisingly, despite tremendous developments in material sciences, elementary particle physics, space science and technology, genetics, and molecular biology, our understanding of the concept of soul, its meaning, universality, nature, constitution, structure, function, and physical location within body in relation to cosmology, structure of matter, terrestrial environment, physiology, psychology, biochemistry, thought process, concept, nature of memory, and physical behaviour are still not known in a holistic way. The author argues against the old concept of soul taking its permanent residence within the body of an organism from the moment of birth to its death. It has instead been argued that the so-called soul, the de facto electric charge, actually remains in continual connection on its own with the universal consciousness (electric potential continuum) from the moment of conception, gestation, development and birth, and all through life to the last breath by means of the 'electric charge' mediated through millions of ion channels within bodies of living organisms. In a way, it is the same universal electrical energy that mediates our localized individual creation, operation, motivation, sustenance, existence and, finally, destruction. Whenever the physical body of any living organism (from the unicellular bacteria to the most evolved of all species, that is, the human being) is incapacitated for the sustained flow of electric charge/universal consciousness/ionic movements within itself to drive electric currents through specific ion channels in motivating the conscious body, death occurs. Death in any multicellular organism is therefore not an instantaneous process, but a gradual withdrawal of electric flow as a result of progressive closing of ion channels from various organs and parts in a sequential order. The Vedic concept and structural model of the soul, described about 8,000 years ago, has been described, argued, and logically discussed in relation to the modern developments in science and the known facts about life to assert that everything attributed to and described about the qualities and properties of the enigmatic soul are also factually true about the electric charge. Therefore, there is merit in assuming that under dogmatic influences of religious beliefs descended down to us through hundreds of centuries, we have, perhaps, lost courage to introspect/argue/question/review our blind belief and have failed to recognize electric charge to be the de facto soul that indeed drives the entire universe and the living world on the earth irrespective of its terrestrial, aquatic, or plant origins. However, unless a global consensus is built on purely scientific (multidisciplinary) merits, the Vedic concept of soul stands tall and provides a logical, quasi-scientific explanation to satisfy the innate human curiosity about life and what drives the living world. Any discussion or explanation on soul is incomplete without such discussion on another enigmatic concept of rebirth and cycles of rebirth and death. I am obliged and compelled to include another comprehensive article with exclusive focus on the concept of rebirth as an independent chapter, even at the risk of some unavoidable repetitions. Here again, it has been argued that there appears to be an incorrect interpretation on the whole concept of rebirth, as first explicitly described in the *Shrimad Bhagavadgita* and descended down to us through thousands of years without question, introspection, or applying independent mind. Modern science does not support rebirth of an individual from the past. At the same time, it provides ample scope, possibility, explanation, and understanding of an individual being born today through the interaction of self-replicating DNA molecules assisted by epigenetic environmental conditions of growth with characteristics and properties of head, heart, and valour that are nearly identical to someone in the historical past and memories about whom have been kept alive in our records or conscious memory through generations. This is because in accepting rebirth of any individual from the past, we always compare similarities in individual characteristics rather than their physical looks, body structure, or constitution. And such replications of characteristic traits are being routinely done and expressed since millions of years by the self-replication of DNA molecules.

The task of compiling a comprehensive multidisciplinary review article with a purely unbiased scientific outlook about such a complex subject as soul was a daunting task, particularly in view of extremely confusing viewpoints, perceptions, discussions, and interpretations done by thousands of authors who have written volumes on these concepts. Again, millions of people have imbibed into their minds innumerable variations of the descriptions of the concepts of soul and rebirth, acquired from equally diverse surroundings, social background, and grooming in childhood. Today, it is very difficult to expect that all readers will have a uniformly common multidisciplinary scientific training and socio-religious background, comprehension, perception, and understanding, besides willingness to welcome and consider radically different and unorthodox thoughts with courage and convictions. One of the reasons for my writing this book is to induce science-oriented readers and, particularly, the scientists from any discipline to understand logic and reasoning from my point of view. Still, it is hoped that the readers would appreciate the efforts with an unbiased, unprejudiced mind, and read something unconventional. A little effort on their part to apprehend the modern scientific phenomena and their relationships with the living world in order to understand the concepts of soul and rebirth, as described, will facilitate the comprehension of the subject matter of this small book.

This comprehensive review article is a revised, enlarged, and updated version of the original presentation made by me under the similar title at the 88th session of the Indian Philosophical Congress held at Sri Venkateshwara University, Tirupati, Andhra Pradesh, India, 17–19 October 2014. In the meantime, I had voluntarily subjected the prepublication draft of this article for review and comments to several of my scientist colleagues, friends, and well-known authorities in this area of subject specialty and, whereas most of them avoided sending any critical or non-critical comments or opinion, some just appreciated me for the unnecessary thankless job I had undertaken. However, I do not personally feel so. Like any curious individual born into a traditional Hindu family in India, the concepts of soul and rebirth had been a passion for me, and I indeed felt restless in not being able to grasp any clear comprehension about both these enigmatic concepts, despite reading the best of books available on the subject from some of the most eminent scholars since my own childhood. A budding physicist within me and my inner curiosity never left me satisfied, until I attempted to write on these subjects and on the present book. I have always believed that no concepts, ideas, beliefs, or thoughts prevail in human civilizations for thousands of years without reason. But whenever there arises any conflict, confusion, or misinterpretations between concepts held dear to our hearts and the progress in contemporary science, it is the responsibility of the scientists to clear doubts and attempt to remove the misconceptions. The present-day truth has to be woven into a new narrative taking scientifically tested selections from the historical past. This book is an honest attempt made in this direction. And in doing so, I do not claim that all that I have written may be the factual truth in reality, but in the absence of any clear direction, I have laboured to look to our ancient concepts from the point of view of as many scientific disciplines as possible. It is merely an attempt on my part to join the missing scientific links and possibly build a complete picture that I could see. These concepts are still evolving and it is impossible to predict where all this evolution is finally going to end. I am particularly grateful to Shri Sadh Guru Jaggi Vasudev, a renowned philosopher, speaker, writer, and mystic guru, for reading my original article and sending me his blessings, and to Professor Vidya Bhushan Gupta, retired dean of the Indian Institute of Technology, Delhi, a polymer physicist of international standing and currently a devoted follower in the order of Radha Saomi Satsang from Dayal Bagh, Agra for appreciation, admiration, and liking this article. I am also particularly grateful to Professor Dr Ravin Lakshman Thatte, MS, FRCS (Edin.), an internationally acknowledged researcher, and plastic and reconstructive surgeon from Mumbai, and a multidisciplinary, multidimensional thinker, scholar and a writer in his own right on the philosophy of *Dnyaneshwari* and *Gita*, for painstakingly going through each and every word of the manuscript and suggesting vital corrections and editorial changes. I am also grateful to Professor Rupert Sheldrake, a renowned biologist, writer, speaker, and critic from England and originator of the concepts and theories of 'morphogenetic fields, morphic resonance, and morphogenesis', for going through the manuscript and for magnanimously bringing out the fact in precise words, and I quote ' ... that this article indeed contains so much in correlating together many different strands of thought with modern physiology and points to deeper interconnections within physics'. This observation, coming from a biologist (with multidisciplinary background) of the stature of Professor Rupert Sheldrake, is particularly gratifying to me with a sense of fulfilment of a mission in life. Likewise, appreciation received from Professor Dick Frans Swaab, head of department at the Netherland Institute of Neuroscience, University of Amsterdam, Netherland, and a well-known researcher on human brain, has been encouraging. Endowed with a basic master's degree in physics, later a PhD in Fibre Science and Textile Technology and a practical work experience for over 37 years as a practising transmission electron microscope specialist in agricultural research, I am amused to have emerged with a rare combination of capacity and experience with advantage for developing a broad interdisciplinary and multidisciplinary mental canvas. All that exists within the dimensional limits from 10^{-14} to 10^{28} cm, incidentally the known expanse of our universe, interests me with a rare privilege to not only understand but to distinctly see and perceive the undercurrent of universal continuum of creation and connectivity through the artificial disciplinary boundaries. To explore and elucidate deep connections between different phenomena in nature is one of the most exciting and natural instincts of a trained physicist, and I am no exception. I have a great urge to not only know all this for myself, but also an intense desire to tell all about what I have explored to those who are anxious to know. It was therefore thought worthwhile to bring out this small publication for wider dissemination and discussion amongst scholars of oriental and scientific philosophy, and to provoke the younger generation of scholars to critically look to the ancient concepts from a purely scientific point of view. I shall not be surprised if they realize that the ancient rishis from India who lived more than 10,000 years ago were certainly very close to the modern scientific understanding of nature and natural material creation. All we need to do today is to search, reveal, correlate, and reinterpret the hard core camouflaged science from the ancient texts with corresponding modern scientific terminologies. Apparently, what is not rational, logical, or scientifically relevant from the ancient texts needs to be filtered out, and what is relevant needs to be integrated into a continually evolving scientific thought. The task is not an easy one, but certainly not impossible if everyone (particularly scientists from related disciplines) attempts to develop the right kind of mindset and evolve himself/herself in a multidisciplinary mode and understanding. This is just the beginning, and I hope that someone from amongst the readers may take the cue and explore such new concepts from ancient literature and provide them the necessary modern scientific foundation. I am aware that in my attempt to write on such complex subjects as soul and rebirth from a multidisciplinary point of view, some words, terms, entities, and theoretical concepts may appear to be cropping up abruptly in the description without any formal background and introduction to the reader. It is not unlikely that for some readers, for want of a multidisciplinary background, they may appear to be speculative. My own convictions as a professional scientist is that if our theoretical foundations for reasoning are sound, then conclusions on expected lines are speculatively inbuilt within. But this is unavoidable because each conceptual terminology would otherwise require at least a paragraph in its description. And considering the limitations and scope of the present book, this was just not possible to do so. Therefore, I have provided the pertinent list of all the references, literature, and books to which any curious reader may revert for in-depth understanding. At best, I can only assure the readers of this book that I have intended and attempted to explore the scientific foundations behind our ancient concepts of soul and rebirth to the best of my ability, comprehension, and capability of interpretation.

I am privileged and grateful to Professor Dr Ravin Thatte for so kindly agreeing to my request to write a foreword for this book. I could not have found a more appropriate person than him for not only being a medical specialist of repute, but a deep thinker and interpreter in his own right as an authority on the philosophy of *Bhagavadgita* and *Dnyaneshwari* by Sant Dnyaneshwar through extensive writings, books, and series of lectures delivered on various platforms within and outside India.

I am particularly indebted to my wife Mrs Sulochana Anil Moharir, my daughter Mrs Prachi Moharir Bajaj, and to my brothers Mr Vijay Vishnu Moharir and late Professor Dr Vasant Vishnu Moharir for their inputs, necessary encouragement, and for infusing courage and confidence in me which boosted me to indulge into such difficult, socio-psychologically complex, at times controversial, and most often, emotionally challenging concepts, prevalent in human psyche for thousands of years and to share them with those interested in the form of this book. This is a multidisciplinary, purely scientific overview on the subjects of soul and rebirth, perhaps the first of its kind, and it is only the readers who would decide how far I have succeeded in my efforts. I have my pleasure in presenting this book in their hands.

New Delhi   **Anil Vishnu Moharir**
13 December 2016

LIST OF KEY WORDS

A Multidisciplinary Review
Consciousness as an Attribute of Electric Charge
Electric Universe
Energy Matter Relationships
History
Modern Scientific Views
Multidisciplinary Review
Soul–Ancient Concept

LORD DATTATREYA

Lord Dattatreya symbolizes the combined manifestation of the three forces of nature that generate, sustain, and destroy all material creation in the universe. Modern physics recognizes four forces in nature, namely weak interaction, strong interaction, gravitation, and electromagnetism. With weak and strong interactions being essentially of similar kind and nature, except in the range of their operation between subatomic particles present within nuclei of atoms, Lord Dattatreya (composite of Brahma, Vishnu, and Mahesh) represents the factual reality of only three forces which are primarily responsible for creation, sustenance, and destruction of all inanimate and animate material in nature. The operative parts of these three primary forces for action in the Indian philosophy have been depicted and symbolized by their three corresponding female deities, namely, Saraswati with Brahma, Lakshmi with Vishnu, and Parvati with Mahesh or Shiva. Saraswati, the operative counterpart of Brahma, the creator, therefore symbolizes the presiding deity for rhythm, rhythmic periodicity, harmony, peace, tranquillity, learning, wisdom, and knowledge. This is clearly obvious because it is our common experience that no orderly creative work (construction, structure, formation etc.) can ever be accomplished without these requirements being in place. In short, without, harmony, peace, rhythm, knowledge, and wisdom, Brahma cannot create anything. And Brahma is primarily responsible for bringing about every specific material creation from the atoms of only 118 different kinds available in the universe. And all atoms, as the fundamental quantum entity, constitute perpetual harmonic oscillators. Vishnu, the sustainer of creation, represents the highest universal cosmic electric potential energy. Vishnu means one who pervades; one who enters into everything that exists. So he is the transcendent as well as the immanent reality of the universe. He is the inner cause and power by which everything in the universe exists. Higher the potential energy, higher is the capacity to create and perform work (creation), and consequently, higher the scope for generating material wealth. Modern physics tells us that no material structure (animate or inanimate) is possible to exist without electric charge which pervades the entire cosmos. The whole universe today is known to be electrical in nature. That leads me to think that it may indeed be the 'electric charge' that most possibly represents the enigmatic entity called 'soul', which we have been searching for and holding dear to our hearts for thousands of years. It is our common knowledge that even the highest electrostatic potential energy generated needs orderly regulation and control for its flow through step-up or step-down transformers and grid systems for distribution to various locations to make it produce useful work. Therefore, Mahalakshmi or Lakshmi, the counterpart female deity of Vishnu (universal cosmic electrostatic potential energy) obviously symbolizes wealth, because it is only with higher accumulation of potential energy and its controlled regulation that there is any possibility to generate the capacity to perform work and create wealth and prosperity. Lastly, Mahesh or Shiva being the mighty destroyer symbolizes the gravitational force in nature which is often destructive. It is the root cause of the accumulation of matter in the universe and for all disturbances as a result of such accumulation on cosmic scale in the universe. The dormant potential state of this mighty force of nature within human body has been symbolized by the kundalini that lies at the base of the spinal cord. Everything concerned with human spirituality and spiritual life, call it by whatever name, such as samadhi, mahasamadhi, nirvana, moksha, communion, union, kaivalya, liberation, bliss, or tranquillity is related to the awakening of kundalini within the body. Active manifestation of the kundalini force, depending upon the purpose of its use in potential capacity generation, continued sustenance, or abrupt destruction are known respectively by the names of Mahalakshmi, Saraswati, and Parvati. No wonder the female operative counterpart of gravitational force should be represented by the most fearful, ruthless, lightning-like quick, abrupt, and thunderously chaotic deity in action known as Parvati. Other variations of this force are Kali, Mahakali, Chandi, Mahishasura Mardini, or Durga. In the tantric literature, when the kundalini force is awakened but cannot be handled, it is called Kali. When it can be handled and used for some beneficial purpose and we become powerful on account of it, it is known as Durga. Both Kali and Durga because of their unpredictable potential destructive power are the most worshiped, feared, and appeased deities for seeking protection to life and property. Both Kali and Durga are indeed the attributes of inner states of human mind/physiology/psychology and behaviour. (For more detailed description, the readers are directed to read *Kundalini Tantra* by Swami Satyanand Saraswati, Yoga Publication Trust, Munger, Bihar, India.) The trinity of Brahma, Vishnu, and Mahesh (Shiva) along with their female counterparts always remain in operation in nature together in tandem and coherence. In case of any weakening of any one of these three forces under any circumstance, the relatively stronger of the remaining two forces become the dominant one and its effect is visualized in action as per its basic nature. In an attempt to seek the scientific truth and meaning contained in the symbolic representation, observation of the above correlations between the concept of the Lord Dattatreya from the Indian philosophy and the modern theory of the physical structure of matter, we only feel dismayed with owe and nothing else.

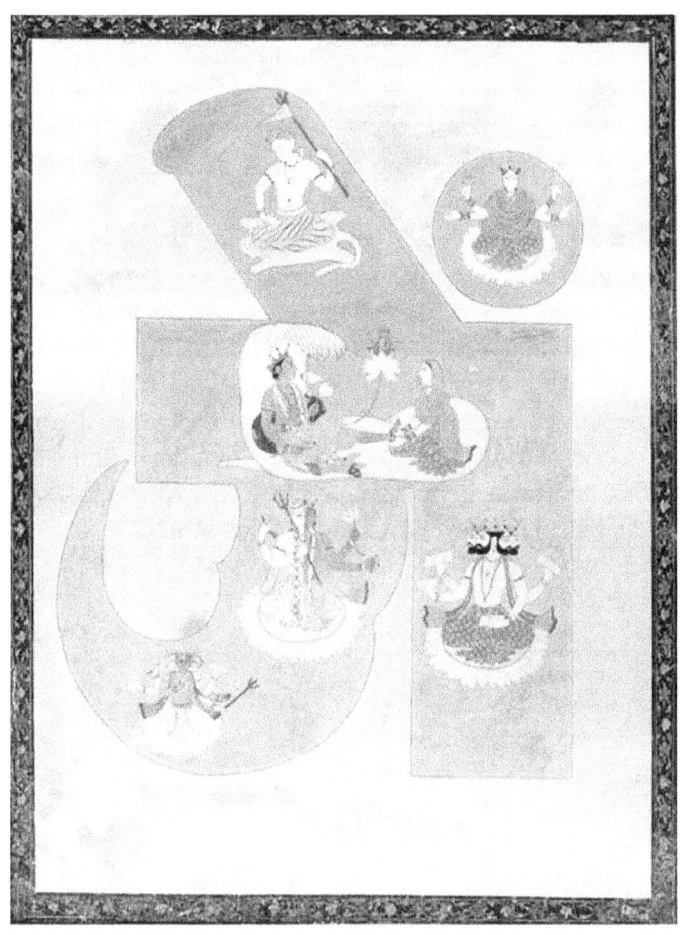

A Pahari painting of an OM containing deities, c.1780-1800.

A Hindu Tantric Painting. India, Pahari, circa 1780–1800. Depicting from top to bottom: Shiva, Sakti, Vishnu on his conch with Brahma sprouting from his navel and Lakshmi, Harihara (Ardha Nari Nateshwara), four-headed Brahma, and the Trimurti (Dattatreya), painted against a gold ground forming the stylized seed syllable Ohm, surrounded by a dark blue floral border with gold painted scrollwork. 12¼ x 9 5/8 in. (31.1 x 24.4 cm)

Source:
http://www.christies.com/LotFinder/search/LOTDETAIL.AS-P?sid=&intObjectID=4346814&SE=CMWCAT03+351845+55
7775189+&QR=M+1+0+Aqc0000900+342345++Aqc0000900
+&entry=india&SU=1&RQ=True&AN=42 (downloaded Aug. 2004)

Brahma–Saraswati, Vishnu–Lakshmi, Shiva–Parvati, and Dattatreya depicted together in the above painting against the background of the primordial harmonically resonating cosmic sound, symbolized by 'Om' and constituting the three fundamental forces in nature, which are responsible for all material creation, their sustenance, and finally destruction in the universe.

Statuette of Ardha-Nari-Nateshwar

As a composite of equal halves of masculine Shiva (left) and feminine Parvati (right). Most possibly, a symbolic representation of the existence of 'supersymmetry' in nature predicted by the modern Standard Model of Particle Physics. For that matter, masculine Brahma and feminine Saraswati, and masculine Vishnu and feminine Lakshmi represents the other two supersymmetric forces of nature.

For discussion, see text under description on 'supersymmetry'.

The above write-up is meant for favour of consideration and introspection by the readers with or without any formal scientific training with the sole objective of arousing scientific curiosity and promoting awareness and attitude to at least attempt to look to our ancient concepts from a purely scientific point of view. In doing so, I may perhaps be incorrect for the time being, but who knows, someone from somewhere, taking this as a clue, may discover and establish the factual scientific truth and understanding behind such ancient concepts.

Anil Vishnu Moharir

Chapter 1

A Scientific Look at the Concept of 'Soul': An Attempted Synthesis

1.1 Abstract

This book traces the developments in the efforts to recognize the difficulties encountered in understanding the enigmatic phenomenon of 'soul', life after death, and reincarnation being discussed for over 5,000 years of human history, and yet being far away from a global consensus. The reasons are more of religious dogma, religious pride, religious divide, blind faith, false sense of superiority of one religion over others, and perhaps above all, fear and lack of courage on the part of people to cross the carefully erected religious and social barriers arising out of metanarrative books and their interpretations to rebel as against scientific logic, reason, arguments, and truth. Despite tremendous developments in material sciences, elementary particle physics, space science and technology, and modern molecular biology, our understanding of the enigmatic concept of soul, its meaning, nature, constitution, structure, function, and physical location within the body in relation to environment, physiology, psychology, biochemistry, thought process, concept and nature of memory, and physical behaviour are still not known in a holistic way. The author argues against the old concept of soul, taking its permanent residence within the body of an organism from the moment of birth till it exits on death. It has been logically argued that instead of taking a permanent residence inside a body, the so-called conscious individual soul actually remains in continual connection on its own with the universal consciousness (electric potential continuum) from the moment of conception, development, birth through its entire life span until its death by means of 'electric charge' mediated through millions of ion channels in the bodies of living organisms. Whenever the physical body of any living organism from the unicellular bacteria to the most evolved of all species, that is, the human being, is incapacitated for the sustained flow of electric charge/ universal consciousness/ionic movements within itself to drive electric currents through specific ion channels in motivating the conscious body, death occurs. Death, at least in any multicellular organism, is therefore not an instantaneous process, but a gradual withdrawal of consciousness as a result of progressive closing of ion channels from various organs/ parts in a sequential order. The Vedic concept and structural model for the soul, described about 8,000 years ago, has been briefly recounted and logically discussed in relation to the developments in modern physical and biological science and the known facts of life to assert that everything attributed to and described about the qualities and properties of the so-called soul are also factually true about the electric charge. Therefore, there is merit in assuming that under the dogmatic influences of religious beliefs descended down to us through hundreds of centuries and repeated by millions of influential religious preachers and stalwarts through the millennial of historical past, we have perhaps lost courage to neither question/review/logically argue nor introspect, and failed to recognize electric charge to be the de facto soul, which not only drives the entire universe but also the living matter on earth, irrespective of its terrestrial, aquatic, or plant origins. However, until a global consensus is built up on scientific merits, the Vedic concept of soul stands tall and provides a logical, quasi-scientific explanation to satisfy human curiosity to a great extent. The task of compiling a comprehensive review article with a purely scientific outlook about such a complex subject as soul from a multidisciplinary point of view was a daunting task. In doing so, it is very difficult to expect that all the readers of this book will have a uniformly common multidisciplinary and socio-religious background, comprehension, and understanding, besides willingness to welcome and consider radically new thoughts on the ancient concepts. Still, it is believed that the readers in general, and the scientific community, in particular, would appreciate the efforts with an open, unbiased mind and read something unconventional because it is not so easy for any individual to break away from our dogmatic emotional views, ideas and prejudices, acquired and held dear to the heart since childhood.

1.2 Introduction and Background Information

Scientific explorations at mental and spiritual levels had begun ever since human beings learnt to observe, think, and analytically interact with their surroundings. This period, on the basis of authentic recorded history, dates back to at least 25,000 C.E. in India during the Vedic civilization. This also initiated in human beings a quest for an understanding of their own position and purpose within the scheme of natural material creation. Man began to explore who he actually is. What is his constitution and composition? Where from and how has he come into being? What is his relation with the other living species on earth? What is the purpose of his existence? What is his final destination? Where is that destination located? And out of several apparently deceptive self-images, what is his real identity? What is materially common between him and surrounding life forms and other lifeless objects? From his birth to deathbed, he observed several irreversibly changing phases in his own life. But the so-called 'I' or 'me' within the frame of his body from birth to death has been believed to have remained the same despite drastic changes in external appearance with time and age. Who is this 'I' or 'me' inside the body? Why is there death and birth? What is the meaning of 'death' and that of 'birth'? Modern developments in physical science tell us that everything in the universe is made up of atoms, the smallest particles of matter which exist in 118 different specific kinds.

The atoms are built up from sub-atomic particles, the protons, neutrons, and electrons, which in turn come about from the elementary particles originating from energy of the magnetic monopoles. Two or more similar or dissimilar atoms combine together with the help of their negatively charged electrons to form structures of various kinds, nature, characteristics, and properties, and they include both the animate and the inanimate world. After a specific period of time, or, under specific environmental conditions, all these animate and the inanimate structures naturally disintegrate into their individual component atoms or groups of atoms to return to nature and are reused or recycled to form new entities. This cycle of formation of structures and their disintegration is continuing in a perpetual way because of the infinite types of energy that abound in 'space' ever since and even before the material universe came into being. This 'space' can be atomic, molecular, planetary, galactic, or universal. The energy undoubtedly is limitless and unending. Recycling of material formed by the chemical combination of various kinds of atoms is the universal law of nature and can only be explained with practical examples. The real miraculous recycling is exemplified by the subtle occurrences that take place within each living organism on this earth. The most efficient chemical recycling in nature takes place between the plants and animals, and in the miracle of the rebirth of essential gases to start the cycle of life via the solar photonic rays. We now know for sure that it is the number of neutrons, positive protons, and negatively charged electrons that provide consciousness, individual identity, integrity, and existence to each of the 118 kinds of atoms as to who they are. And it is the atoms which are perpetually recycled in nature. Obviously therefore, the concept of a definite lifespan, fate, and destiny must have emerged from the varying intervals of time observed for different materials (both animate and inanimate) between the moment of their creation to their disintegration. Everything in the universe from movement of stellar constellations to galaxies, planets and planetary motions, rotation of earth and its moon around the sun to occurrence of the day and night cycles as well as the seasons on earth are, therefore, observed to be cyclic and periodic. Like every other phenomenon in nature, it was but natural to also ask if events like 'death' and 'birth' of animate objects in nature are also cyclic. So far as the question of all animate organisms as a part of the natural material creation is concerned, recycling of their constituent material after death is well understood. But, if every individual (and in this context, possibly every kind of life form) is also destined to return back to birth in a cyclic phase after their death, as is popularly believed, then obviously a series of other questions come to mind. How? When? Where? Which form and sex of a living being? And after what interval of time is this return possible? What are the conditions that determine our return in a rebirth? And most importantly, whether those conditions are self-organized, and if not, then by whom or under what physical or environmental circumstances does that happen? What happens to the 'I' or the 'me' in the body? Is this identity carried forward to the next birth? While in a majority of cases children forget and do not remember the identity of their past life, thousands of case studies have been recorded from all over the world wherein children, predominantly in the age group of 2–6 years, distinctly remember their past births. Where does this 'I' or 'me' stay after death and in what form and conditions? What is conscious memory about the 'I' or the 'me' and what is its vehicle? How and where this memory is located, gets recorded, and recalled? What or who keeps record of this memory? Is it recorded by the 'I' or 'me' (as metaphysical entity) that is believed to live within the body or by any of the several organ parts of the body? When bodies from the past lives are physically burned or destroyed, how, then, does the memory get transported and recalled after rebirth, as has been observed and reported from all parts of the world? Obviously therefore, memory cannot be something materially physical. And for that matter, the possibility of genes (DNA) carrying the memory (of conscious individual identity) is scientifically impossible, because genetic memory essentially requires an unbroken physical transfer of genetic material from one life to another of the same individual. Scientific observation and logic about past-birth memory indicates that genetic explanation for transfer of memory from one life to the next is not possible. Obviously, it can be assumed that it may be the non-destructible, metaphysical entities 'I' or 'me' within bodies that must be carrying memories of past births with it. And if this is so, then it is curious to know the structure, form, and make-up of this so-called 'I' or 'me', and where and how the memories of life are stored and recorded within it and transported to the following births. These questions have been repeatedly raised by philosophers, thinkers, religious leaders, and research scientists since thousands of years of human history without coming to a definite, unanimous, and universally accepted answer. *Actually, a few thousand isolated cases of individuals claiming to remember their past births are statistically insignificant or negligible in comparison to several billions of others who just do not remember anything of their past lives.* Howsoever insignificant, it is a tribute to the integrity of the scientist community that they do not want to leave anything for chance and every single anamorphous incidence is subjected to a rigorous scientific scrutiny. Yet, there is no conclusive scientific proof of rebirths being evident. Still, if we claim or intuitively feel that some form of identity as 'soul' persists beyond death, it becomes necessary to know what stuff or particles is that soul made of? Is it materialistic or non-materialistic by nature? Is it real or merely an illusion? What kind of forces hold it together within a body and allow it to exhibit its conscious attributes? And how does it interact with ordinary matter? These are some of the questions that need to be explained on the basis of scientific reason and logic. Alternately, a logical explanation for the origin, assembly, manifestation, reproduction, and exhibition of all attributes of conscious living beings has to be found and explained from the characteristics, properties, and behaviour of their constituent atomic or molecular material, and we should be open to consider, discuss, and accept such new interpretations.

William Grassie[1] argues that there is a deep narrative structure of human thought and it is through this narrative that we create and recreate our selfhood, and that the 'self' is a product of our telling and not some essence to be delved in the recesses of subjectivity. Narratives not only create the inner and social selves for individuals; narratives also bind societies and cultures together by inducing similar thoughts and thereby creating similar ideologies. They help us to integrate events and actions over a period of time into meaningful patterns, specify cause and effect relationships, and organize them into coherent wholes. It is the narratives which tell us which events and actions are significant and which can be ignored. The narratives again explain the interrelationships of all events in our lives. Our moral reasoning is not a matter of our propositional logic and rational choice, but a product based on the analogical application of powerful narrative stories (fed to our imagination in our grooming from childhood) to new situations in the course of our life. In short, it is only the exercise in a certain nesting of stories and stories within stories together all the way down. The most important stories which humans tell, retell, reframe, and circulate for generations are not even consciously recognized at all to be only stories. These master stories, called the metanarratives, are the stuff of ideologies, religions, nationalisms, faiths, sects, and cultures that form the unarticulated background,

1 William Grassie, Chapter 7 in The New Science of Religion: Exploring Spirituality from the Outside In and Bottom Up (New York: Palgrave Macmillan, 2010)

emotional modulations, and conditioning of our 'taken-for-granted truth'. And once captured and entrenched in the minds of people, these metanarratives become difficult to be rationalized or refuted. They structure our thoughts, personality, beliefs, and behaviour in many profound ways. It is this background which is responsible for our prejudices, biases, and social choices. In general, people surrender their ability to doubt and think independently for themselves. No wonder why discussions on religion or politics between people with widely different beliefs very often generate heat, rage, and even violence. By virtue of habit, people tend to choose facts based on metanarratives and carefully interpret them to new situations. No surprise, therefore, that whenever metanarrative books have been forbidden for updating, revision, editing, correction, or a new interpretation in the light of advancements in science and technology, there follows a certain confusion, frustration, regimentation, irrationality, and obstinate adherence to ritualistic traditions and intolerance amongst their believers and followers.

1.3 Necessity of a Scientific Theory for Life after Death or Reincarnation

In this connection, from times immemorial, several theories have been proposed and explanations given by many persons from all over the world, but, surprisingly, not a single theory enjoys universal acceptance. Natural laws of creation of the living world and the process of birth and death in humans are universally common, irrespective of physical location on the earth, environmental, and climatic conditions at the place of birth, colour of skin, race, blood group type, level of education or literacy, and such other considerations. In this respect, therefore, there are no separate laws for different nationalities, communities, or races. The science of human birth and death does not recognize differences between religious faiths because the structural make-up and the kind of various organs, physical appearance and forms, physiological, biochemical, metabolic, mental, emotional, and psychological thought processes are identical, irrespective of location, colour of skin, and external features. Not a single case of sexual infertility has ever been reported from marriages between partners observing different religious faiths. If there are natural scientific laws which can be logically and adequately used within statistical limits of accuracy and probability to understand and explain the entire process of creation, properties, functions, differences, corrective measures, and sustainability of the living and non-living material world, then there is no reason why a universally acceptable theory or explanation cannot be sought or arrived at on questions regarding life, its origin, death, birth, and rebirth, for the entire community of conscious living organisms (inclusive of all unicellular, multicellular, and multi-organ organisms) shares a common gene pool, planet for heritage, dwelling, and destiny. Such a theory should however be based purely on merits of scientific truth, logic, reason, and free from dogmatic personal or social bias towards religious opinions, blind faiths, allegiance, influence, prejudice, or any other commercial or social vested interest. Even Albert Einstein admitted that: 'We believe that science serves humanity best when it is all free of influence by any dogma and reserves the right to question all assumptions, including their own', and 'it is more difficult to break a prejudice than an atom'.

Human beings observe and follow a particular faith or religion, mainly because of parental nurture and grooming in childhood, and also a certain family or social structure rather than as an independently chosen personal option. Once adapted to a particular thought or a ritual, it stays as a habit with the person throughout his/her life. More particularly, faiths in general are being mechanically followed as unconscious victims of mob psychology, or, more particularly, due to morphic resonance of social morphic fields, as described by Rupert Sheldrake, and arising out of strong community feelings and identity, sense of insecurity, a constant fear of something unknown, lack of self-confidence, lack of freedom and courage to cross social structural and ideological boundaries, and incapacity for independent thinking to reason outside the frame of grooming since birth. These fields interact with each other among different individual members of the same species and are the reasons for a collective coordinated behaviour of individual members, for example, coordinated formation of birds during flights, swimming of fish in schools, behaviour of individual human beings in a crowd, etc. Sheldrake theorizes that living morphic fields simultaneously exist in the past, present, and future and govern both human and animal behaviour, forming a living matrix upon which the physical bodies are formed. Therefore, such conscious or unconscious victimization and submission to mechanical, ritualistic following of any religion/faith is visible in all communities across the world and has been very well documented by Richard Dawkins and Robert Hinde, as a result of his Gallup poll in the United States in which three quarters of staunch Catholics and Protestants could not name a single Old Testament prophet, more than two-thirds did not know who preached the sermon on the mount, and an equal number thought that Mosses was one of the twelve apostles of Jesus. A similar situation exists amongst the followers of all other faiths or religions.

Many faiths such as Christianity and Islam (with a common origin) deny the possibility of human life after death or rebirth more as a religious dogma than for any sound scientific logic, despite the holy book being known to be an axiom and not the end product of a process of scientific reasoning. And yet, the book was always vehemently upheld to be true. Moreover, in some cases where the evidence seemed to contradict it, it is the evidence that was preferred to be thoughtlessly thrown out without question, reason, or introspection and not the book. It is a historical fact that reincarnation was an accepted part of Judaism into which

Jesus himself was born. The original texts of both the Old and the New Testaments indeed contained references to life after death and reincarnation, but they were consciously and deliberately removed in AD 325 by the Roman emperor, Constantine the Great, and his mother Helena. The Second Ecumenical Council of Constantinople meeting in AD 553 confirmed and endorsed their action, declaring the concept of reincarnation as a heresy, but, more objectively, as a possible ulterior threat to the growing power and hegemony of the Church if people were allowed to logically think and keep independent opinions. The scientific truth that earth was not the centre of the universe was opposed for hundreds of years by the dogmatic Christian Church, purely on blind faith. Eminent independent thinkers who opposed the view of the Church were compelled to abandon their views and opinions, persecuted, tortured, or forced to drink poison and accept death. No wonder, universal unanimous acceptability for any scientifically logical theory on soul, rebirth, or life after death has always been made difficult, not because there is no such theory in existence which logically attempts to explain all the phenomenon mentioned above, but only because our social, political, and religious leaders from all nationalities, since time immemorial, consciously or unconsciously, purposefully or otherwise, have been only dividing humanity into factions of races and groups of religious faiths in the name of supremacy of one faith over others and, thereby, setting individuals against accepting such a theory in the name of faith or allegiance or loyalty to a religion that does not subscribe to such ideas and, more particularly, for fear of inviting wrath of the mighty powerful ruler or the unknown God as a creator. Therefore, for the time being, there are no relevant reasons for either accepting or summarily rejecting the concept of soul or reincarnation, until they are thoroughly contested on the basis of modern scientific logic and reason. They continue to be a question of blind dogmatic faith, belief and disbelief, a mental block, vested interest, or lack of conviction and courage to impartially uphold a possible logical scientific truth.

For instance, Christianity did not subscribe to earth being an ordinary planet that revolves around the sun, but had to abandon its dogma because they could no longer hold people bound to their views against scientific truth and logic. The sole purpose in doing all this was to sow seeds of confusion, kill the capacity and initiatives of individuals for independent thinking and judicious evaluation based on scientific reason and logic, besides imposing curbs on intellectual freedom by way of polarizing the minds of the lay population. No wonder, there have been innumerable cases of coercion, regimentation, detentions, engineered riots, physical killing, and eliminations of those who rebelled against such orthodox systems put in place by vested socio-economic-religious power groups. The very fact that both Christianity and Islam, right from the time they attempted to propagate professional religion, did not advocate belief in rebirth as a basic tenet of their philosophy, not much thinking was either allowed to be done in this direction, or it was physically curbed or actively destroyed by the followers of both these faiths. It is also a well-known historical fact that both Christianity and Islam have been propagated more on the might of the sword and dogmatism. This is exemplified by Edgar Cayce, a psychic clairvoyant, who would place himself into a self-hypnotic trance to give healing relief to mentally and psychologically disturbed people, and was convinced that the reasons for a specific condition of a person was mainly due to memories of his/her past life influences. Despite this self-realization, Edgar Cayce, who was a devout Christian by faith, did not dare to honestly profess or conscientiously share his self-realized truth in public, but merely confined himself to silently practising 'life readings' of affected people. Today, more and more people from the Western world, and about 30 per cent people in the United States, despite their faith in Christianity, believe in life after death and reincarnation.

Sufis, the esoteric branch of Islam and Hasidic Judaism, support reincarnation, and so also the Gnostic and mystical traditions of Christianity. Outside the religion, Pythagoras, Plato, David Hume, Ralph Waldo Emerson, Henry Thoreau, Benjamin Franklin, J.W. von Goethe, and Sir Isaac Newton all were known to have believed in reincarnation.

Hypnotic regression (which is supposedly believed to make patients remember their past births) is being increasingly used these days by psychologists and psychotherapists as a regular therapy to cure patients ridden with chronic mental depression, hallucinations, fear, and traumatic phobia of knives, rivers, oceans and water bodies, mountain heights, vehicles, trains, aeroplanes, and such other problems with successful return of their patients to live their normal lives after erasing the causative metabolic, physiological or genetic reasons, or memory of their fear and phobia believed to have been inherited from their past lives. Not only this, when hypnotically regressed into their past memories (lives), people at times have been reported to speak in languages completely unknown to them in the present lives. In this context, Marcus Tillius Cicero (106–43 BC), the Roman philosopher, maintained that the fact our children grasp certain abilities and skills at surprising speeds is a strong proof of their knowing those skills before birth, and that genius is nothing but only the flowering of experience from the previous life. Such abilities in picking knowledge and learning find an easy explanation in the theory of life after death. Similarly, the reasons for differences in aptitude and abilities between children (including twins) born to same parents with identical genetic heritage may have an explanation in the hypothesis of life after death. If this is true, then it remains to understand how incidental memories, experiences, and skills acquired in previous lives are transferred to the present life without physical transfer of the genetic molecule DNA through successive procreations. Perhaps, we need to relook at the

DNA, its anti-parallel asymmetric structure, their number in each organism, its types, process of replication, operation, function, or some hidden dimensions (if any) of these self-replicating molecules of life from an entirely different perspective[2]. There appears to be some other (hitherto unknown) mode for transfer of memories, information, experiences, and skills from one generation to the other. And this process may altogether be independent of the structural make-up of the DNA, and even more likely, without physical necessity of rebirth of an individual as a precondition. Intensive polarization of thoughts within groups of persons through repeated dialogues, discussions, and discourses with influential preachers or by reading emotionally captivating metanarrative books are some of the most important modes for transfer of memories to multiple individuals. Therefore, alternately, the role of the morphic fields and their resonance that simultaneously transcend through the past, present, and future in the transfer of memory, experience, and skill, as proposed by Rupert Sheldrake, deserve a far more serious consideration. Fields, resonances, and their causative effects on matter and its behaviour can be easily correlated with the fundamental nature, properties, and characteristic vibrations of the atoms and molecules from which the entire universe (both animate and inanimate) has come into being. Questions about our continued belief in the theory of rebirth have recently been critically discussed by the author of this book elsewhere, and the same has also been included as an independent chapter in this book. On the other hand, Professor Dick Frans Swaab, a researcher of international repute on human brain[3], indicates that all phenomena such as NDE (near-death experiences), re-experiencing panoramic memories of events that had taken place several

2 Subhash Kak, 2006, *Garbha Upanishad* (translation and notes by the author).
3 Dick Swaab, *We are our Brains: From the Womb to Alzheimer's* (London: Penguin Books, 2014) (trans. by Jane Headley-Prole).

decades earlier in the past, epilepsy, experiencing spiritual or religious feelings of being in unison with universe, world, or God, thoughts of having gone to heaven, or experiencing the feeling of being in direct contact with God, Jesus, or some other religious figure, the feeling of peace and tranquillity, absence of pain, the vision of going through a long tunnel, and all such experiences are in fact the results of some kind of impairment of brain function, inducing a state between consciousness and deep sleep and unconsciousness. Several other reasons such as severe blood loss, septic or anaphylactic shock (severe allergic reactions), electrocution, going into coma due to brain damage or cerebrovascular accident, suicide, near-drowning and depression, excessive levels of carbon dioxide, hyperventilation, lysergic acid diethylamide (LSD), psilocybin or mescaline (hallucinogens), and sudden acceleration to higher altitudes in fighter jet planes have also been reported to induce such experiences. An out-of-body experience can be triggered by stimulating the place where the temporal lobe and the parietal lobe meet in the brain. Use of cannabis triggers a great many chemical reactions in the brain and electrical stimulation near the fornix at the rear of the hypothalamus gland also activates the experience of recalling events that had taken place several decades earlier. This area has been earmarked to be storing episodic autobiographical memories that form the chronicle of our lives. Moreover, being extremely sensitive to lack of oxygen, it can easily be activated. Likewise, stimulation of hippocampus provokes extremely clear, highly detailed autobiographical memories, including memories of people who have died.

1.4 Dawn of the Scientific and Industrial Revolution and Implications

The dawn of modern scientific and industrial revolution in the closing years of the nineteenth century initiated an assertive process of definition, evaluation, and calibration of all units of physical quantities and their measurement, followed by universal standardization of material characterization, applications, and mass industrial production with a consequent improvement in the quality of human life. These developments have led to accepting and adopting science and technology as the vehicles of change for economic prosperity, reducing inequalities and global socialization. The scientific thought process founded on the philosophical basis of Rene Descartes, Lord Francis Bacon's methodology, and Sir Isaac Newton's mathematics, supported by experimental verification on the basis of logically built hypothesis and theories for explaining any natural phenomena have become the foundations of state policies, besides ensuring quality of governance and livelihood support to citizens at affordable costs. These efforts have not only gone in organizing material natural resources, but also in harnessing the seemingly invisible resources in the form of nuclear, space, communication, digital and nanoscience technologies. Today, no one questions or doubts the potential, power, utility, and practical application value of physical gadgets that are spinning out from these sciences concerning the invisible but realistic sub-atomic world. A new era of scientific awareness, willingness to change with an open mind for accepting new thoughts, new sciences, and new possibilities with consideration and respect for plausible alternate explanations for the known phenomena has dawned. Subjects like consciousness, mind, mind–matter interface and interactions, thoughts and thought waves, their teleportation to distant location, telepathy, distant vision, clairvoyance, precognition, psychokinesis, near-death experiences, after death reincarnation, bioelectronics, paraphysics, and parapsychology etc. which were contemptuously held unscientific are no longer forbidden from scientific exploration and enquiry. Because of developments in science in the twentieth century, scientists are increasingly getting aware of the universal continuum of information, knowledge, interconnectivity of sciences, and the innumerable possibilities of energy–matter interactions and their manifestation as realities. Thanks to the scientific reconfirmation that man is a part and parcel of nature and the entire universe contributes to our life and to what we are, coming through the information gathered with the help of interplanetary and galactic probes and the Hubble Space Telescope. Scientists are far more willing, without any aversion or prejudice, now to experimentally explore these areas, and conservative agencies are even encouraging research with lavish funding. There is, therefore, no reason or justification for religious leaders or preachers to remain ignorant, aloof, isolated, or blinded about these developments or to keep their followers scientifically unaware and ignorant, and continue to dogmatically oppose new thinking. They first need to broaden their mindset themselves, develop capacity to understand and correlate the new science, evolve with changing time, accept reality, and help in providing a scientific basis to the preaching of their faiths (metanarratives) to newer generations. Because, the only purpose of all religions is to individually and collectively educate and empower their followers to live mentally, emotionally, thoughtfully, intellectually, physiologically, nutritionally, and physically in sound health, and, above all, socially in harmony with the laws of nature. Depending upon the geographical location on earth, our food intake, its nature, and effective digestion, the metabolisms of our bodies are mediated to a great extent by the external environment, and religious preachers must help their followers in developing the necessary mental strategies to deal with them for a healthy survival. This is the only meaning, essence, purpose, and duty of all religions, past or present that have flourished on the earth. Perhaps, this may have been the reason why Sir Isaac Newton, emotionally took to preaching religion (scientific) at the fag end of his career in science and mathematics. He is reported to have been appealing for drastic reformation of religion in the practise of the most essential common activity, the human worship of God. There is, therefore, no scope, logic, reason, wisdom, and purpose to pitch one religion or faith against another as rivals. Science and inculcation of scientific attitude is going to be the only new religion of the world, irrespective of geographical location or nationalities. No wonder, there appears some truth in the statement of Acharya Rajneesh Osho, when he said: 'If religions (old) do not progressively evolve with the time and modern scientific thoughts, they will have no option but to die.'

1.5 Everything in the Universe Is Made of Atoms: Recycling Is the Fundamental Law of Nature

Hydrogen, as the basic element in nature, constitutes about 80 per cent of our universe. With only one proton and one electron, the nuclei of hydrogen atoms fuse together to produce all other heavier elements found in nature. As the basic element and building blocks from which nuclei of all other 118 different kinds of atomic elements are derived, hydrogen expresses the oneness and universal continuum and all other expressions can be reduced to that oneness. However, the exceptional moment that marked the starting point of the development, that is, the formation and proliferation of hydrogen in the universe from something that did not materially exist and the conditions that triggered this continues to baffle scientists to date. Hydrogen (proton with unit positive electric charge) corresponds exactly to the cosmic energy of that very moment when the 'hydrogen proton' as the first atomic or sub-atomic material came into being. In other words, hydrogen is the connecting link in the process of unification with the origin and cosmic centre and the enigmatic soul believed to be manifesting within the living material unit, the biological cell. It also implies a recognition and awareness of the fact that we are all one with the integration of this cosmic energy at the cellular level. Perhaps, the mystery of local and universal consciousness is hidden in the way hydrogen fosters, sustains, maintains, and, of course, mediates the formation of structures through chemical covalent bonds with itself or with any other kinds of elemental atoms, obviously through its negative equivalent of electric charge, the electron. The so-called valence electrons of an elemental atom are the real workhorse of all the electrons orbiting its nuclei. These valence electrons interact with other valence electrons of another atom nearby to foster ionic or covalent bonds between themselves. Ionic bonds are formed as result of transfer of electron from one atom to the other, whereas their sharing between the two atoms forms what are called the covalent bonds. Most organic plants and animal substances are formed basically through the carbon atom (C), which creates stable linkages with other atoms such as carbon, oxygen, hydrogen, and nitrogen by sharing each other's electrons through covalent bonds. Essentially, this process needs sunlight for their formation. Almost 99 per cent of the atoms in the conscious organic life systems on the earth are made up of carbon, hydrogen, oxygen, and nitrogen. But, as a result of the infinite number of compounds involved, organic life is very complex. Vegetation, which proliferates with carbon dioxide (CO_2) and water (H_2O) in the presence of photonic energy from the sun, is the starting point of the whole cycle of animate material creation. This solar photonic energy gets translated into adenosine triphosphate (ATP) in the process of photosynthesis in plants and in the hydrolysis of carbohydrates in all animals. Thus, ATP molecules, tracing their origin from the solar energy, in fact, motivate all plant and animal life forms on the earth. All these plant and other life forms, from the moment of birth to the last breath, only lead a struggle to receive solar energy for their survival. No wonder, the reason as James Morgia describes: 'Why everything on this planet earth raises its branches and arms to the Sun.' This has been going on since times immemorial, yet, no one knows how it happens. It is only the negatively charged electron which knows how and why it happens, and also the true meaning and purpose of recycling of material in nature. Therefore, most probably, we may have failed to recognize 'hydrogen proton' or its negative equivalent the 'electron', that is, the electric charge to be the *de-facto* soul and lost ourselves in the mire of confusion created by our fanciful invention, description, and adventure of assigning arbitrary attributes to several terminologies, such as I/me/self/soul/psyche/astral body/conscience/subtle body/spirit/subconscious/superconscious/voice of the heart/ atma/paramatma/energy-informational matrix/reactive mind or a quantum monad, etc. in essentially describing the same thing popularly known since antiquity as the soul. It is worth standing away from the madding crowd and orthodox views, pause for a while, and introspect, if our efforts to realize the enigmatic soul may not be a proverbial 'chase for the wild goose'.

We now know that the electron is not only the carrier of negative electric charge, but it is also the least massive of the three particulate constituents (electron, proton, and neutron) of all atoms. Particles with masses lower than that of an electron have no electric charge, which implies that if the electron was to somehow decay in a hypothetical situation, it must lose its charge altogether. This would mean a clear violation of the 'principle of conservation of electric charge' and would not be acceptable. A pertinent search for the observation of electron decay in the Borexino detector experiments in Italy has not seen the faintest evidence. On the contrary, the charge on an electron is not only confirmed to be quantized, but universally stable with a life time of at least 66,000 yottayears (6.6 X 10^{28} years) (a time period, which is five quintillion times the current age of the universe itself[4]). This is the reason that the electron is considered to be a fundamental particle, which never decays. If the electric charge indeed represents the *de facto* enigmatic 'soul', as has

---

4 See Hamish Johnston, 2015, electron lifetime is at least 66,000 yottayears, Editor Physicsworld.com. (http:// www. theamericanscholar.org/a-new-theory-of-the-universe).

been discussed and argued earlier, then such a long stability of electrons for over 10^{28-31} years also explains why the so-called 'souls' have been resolutely believed and justified to be indestructible in all religious philosophies that have flourished in the history of human civilizations.

G.W. Warder in his celebrated book *The Universe a Vast Electric Organism* also mentions that electric charge is the invisible force which evolves from substance and all visible things. Matter is but the outer garment of these invisible electric forces. It is the spirit (the so-called soul/electric charge—my interpretation) which creates psychic life and makes life the cause instead of the consequence of organisms. Sir J.J. Thompson while announcing the discovery of electrons also described them as the common constituent of all matter. The flow of electrons is called the electricity or electric current. It is electricity which has evolved the physical universe and makes it a vast electric organism bound together by invisible electrical forces. Against such a background of historical developments in this area of subject matter, most of the descriptive (metanarrative) texts on soul contributed by eminent persons over centuries in the past from various disciplines are indeed a myriad collection of beautifully worded, strongly motivating, emotionally charged, intricately skilled, psychologically captivating, thoughtfully polarizing, mentally paralyzing, yet, profoundly influential literary compositions of scintillating words and phrases, subjectively presenting individual perceptions of these authors/compilers, and lacking in scientific clarity and details.

Everything in the animate and inanimate material world is made up of atoms, the basic units as 'energy condensates' and building blocks of matter that were created in nuclear furnaces of developing stars about 13.7 billion years ago, and are universally available in very limited number of kinds and quantity. Ever since, the particulate atoms have maintained their identities and individual characteristics.

Perhaps, the invariable and incorruptible values of the 200+ odd 'physical constants' in nature have maintained the individual identities of these element atoms. Why and how the values of these physical constants are so finely and precisely tuned that makes the existence of the material universe and conscious life forms possible on earth is a perpetual unsolved mystery. We have no means or capacity to alter their values, and certainly no option but to accept them as they are. It is even more impossible to know if the origin of the (200+) physical constants precede the origin of atomic matter in the universe or vice versa. Or both might have evolved simultaneously together and got mutually tuned? Halit Eroglu has recently derived all fundamental physical constants from a new formula ($ℏ.c$ = square root of 10) discovered by him in addition to some very interesting correlations in the quantum world. The factor of time and the quantized values are held to be responsible for the dynamics of natural constants. According to Eroglu, 'Like all other physical quantities "time" is also quantized and all interactions between quantized sizes take place in accordance to quantized timing cycles'. The bizarre precise tuning of the values of 200+ physical constants is believed by some to be the handiwork of an outside super intelligent creator. But superintelligence is inherently ingrained in itself—in the structure, composition, characteristics, properties, function, and behaviour of all the atoms of various kinds. There is, therefore, no need for any other external superintelligence as a creator. Even a slight change in the value of any one of these physical constants would have made the existence of the universe and conscious matter impossible. Under the scheme of such a universal material creation when the universe came into being or the proverbial 'Big Bang' occurred, there is also a speculative possibility to assume that a highly energetic, mysteriously constituted 'conscious-quantum-particulate-entity' called the soul/quantum monad with individual characteristic identity, similar to those of the atoms, were also simultaneously created from the primordial cosmic energy and manifested as living organisms, only after favourable environmental conditions such as those on the earth were found. If true, then it does not rule out the presence of such 'quantized potential souls' everywhere in the universe and certainly their transportation to the earth from outer space, a possibility. Coupling and connecting with them from earth is therefore only a matter of tuning and matching our inherent energy frequency and establishing a harmonic resonance. Such a possibility and capacity within the human body indeed exists and has been demonstrated by several saints and rishis. Researches in the area of exobiology and extraterrestrial origin of life also confirm the creation, origin, sustenance, and existence of biomolecules within the intervening medium of our solar system and intergalactic space. Curiously enough, all biomolecules, like the atoms, indeed form quantum entities with similar characteristics, for example, spin, vibrations, frequencies, and electrical charge distribution along their molecular-chain-length and polar ends. Studies on quantum interactions in biological molecules conducted by researchers from the Weizmann Institute have recently shown that DNA molecules are extremely sensitive to electron spin and can discern and filter the electrons moving through them. However, as long as the mystery about the 'primordial cosmic energy' remains scientifically unresolved, so long the mystery about the constitution and composition of the soul will remain shrouded in the realm of spiritual ambiguity. Perhaps, the newer experiments planned beyond the recent discovery of Higgs Boson, the proverbial 'god particle', from the Large Hadron Collider (LHC) accelerator may reveal some deeper clues. For the first time in the history of particle accelerators and colliders, the LHC will be able to probe beyond the now well-established physics of the Standard Model of Elementary Particle Physics. It will certainly push the theory to discover new physics and lead physicists into a realm hitherto unknown. Having discovered the Higgs particle, the new goal for conducting experiments with the LHC would be to tie the loose ends within the Standard Model and, perhaps, this may require a new theory. For example, according to the Standard Model, particles acquire and possess mass because of the effect of the Higgs force, but it does not explain why different types of particles have different masses. Why a muon particle is 207 times heavier than an electron, or why a top quark is so enormously massive as compared to the other quarks? Further, the Standard Model of Particle Physics cannot explain why there are three generations of elementary matter particles. Another important embarrassing question that the Standard Model of Particle Physics has been unable to resolve is that most of the matter present in the universe appears to consist of an unknown substance which does not emit light and is only known through its gravitational influence on other matter. For this reason, it is known as dark matter. It is believed that dark matter is composed of huge quantities of very weakly interacting relic particles that were produced in prodigious amounts soon after the Big Bang occurred and the universe came into being about 13.7 billion years ago. If this logic and reason is correct, then it is expected that this particle may spring up in experiments, any day, any time in the LHC. Fundamental particles have been classified into two separate classes that display completely different behaviour. One class of particles is the constituents of matter, while the other class of particles mediate the forces that hold matter together. Matter-forming particles such as the electron obey Pauli's 'exclusion principle', which means that each one must be in a different wave state. This curious property is shared by all the fundamental particles from which matter is formed, and they include protons, neutrons, and quarks. In fact, it is this property that enables them to condense into matter and collectively they are known as 'fermions' after Professor Enrico Fermi. Likewise, the particles whose exchange produces a force, such as photons, behave in a completely different way because they exist in the same wave state and form a single wave (for example, Laser). Particles that behave in this way are collectively known as 'bosons' after the Indian physicist Professor Satyendra Nath Bose. The matter and the force-carrying particles could then be paired up with force-carrying particle for each matter particle and vice versa. This is the sort of deep relationship that is believed to be lying at the heart of matter and what the physicists are exactly striving for—a unity that leads to more profound understanding of the universe. Its discovery would represent a major step towards total unification of all the four forces of nature and all the particles within a single theory which has been given the name 'supersymmetry'. Supersymmetry has therefore been described as 'a symmetry between matter-forming particles, such as electrons and quarks, and force-mediating particles, such as photons, gluons and the Higgs'. Supersymmetry is believed to unite the matter and force particles together in a warm, mutual, metaphorically masculine embrace of the sturdy mass particles entwined with the metaphorically feminine force-carrying particles. (*Compare and contrast this scientific fact to the ancient Vedic philosophy of pairing masculine Brahma, Vishnu, and Mahesh with their feminine counterparts, Saraswati, Lakshmi, and Parvati respectively, described in the author's write-up on Lord Dattatreya [Figure 1] as a frontispiece to this book. Further, the theoretical demand of supersymmetry requiring matter-carrying particles and force-carrying particles to essentially have equal amount of electric charge on them for pairing is akin to the concept of 'Ardha-Nari-Nateshwara'—equal halves of Shiva and Parvati in the constitution of human body [Figure 2]).* If the universe is really governed by the supersymmetric laws, then each type of matter-carrying particle needs to have its complementary supersymmetry force-mediating partner. Conversely, each force-mediating particle has a supersymmetric matter-carrying particle. Theoretically, matter-carrying particle and force-carrying particles for supersymmetry pairing must have exactly the same amount of electric charge, but this is not the case for the particles that are currently known to physicists, therefore, all the known particles cannot be paired up in this way. So, if supersymmetry is indeed the symmetry of the real world, then it would imply the existence of many different new particles to be discovered in the years to come. There would be a new superpartner particle with opposite spin property for each known particle. Thus, the spin-1/2 electron is accompanied by a spin-zero selectron, the spin-1 photon by a photino of spin-1/2, the spin-1/2 quark by a spin-zero squark. With the LHC being doubled in energy, in the years to come, we look forward to moving to the next level of our understanding about the nature and constitution of matter. And, physicists, in anticipation of their discovery in the years to come, have already provided suitable names for all such particles. Their suggested names, for instance being, superpartner of photon will be known as 'photino', superpartners of W and Z particles will be known as 'Winos' and 'Zinos', superpartner of gluon as 'gluinos', superpartner of Higgs is 'Higgsino', and that of electron and quark as 'selectron' and 'squark' respectively. Their discovery would reveal the origin of the dark matter so abundantly distributed in the universe[5]. The tremendously ambitious and ultimate goal of theoretical physicists is to find a single theory that encompasses the whole of physics and answers all our fundamental questions about the universe and the material within it. A dream that was inflamed by Albert Einstein. The recent discovery of the 'Higgs particle' is the first greatest achievement in the twenty-first century towards this end. It indeed marks a definitive proof that we all, as conscious organisms, are really living continuously connected within a 'cosmic superconductor'. Perhaps, the nature, manifestation,

5 See also the website of Professor Robert Lanza for details at http://www.robertlanzabiocentrism.com.

and composition of the kind of energy involved in the constitution of that enigmatic, illusive particle what we call by the name of soul/quantum monad/prana/*atma* (if it ever separately exists) may not be known today, but, intuitively enough, it cannot be any different from the perpetual energy-matter interactions going on in the universe at the subtlest level.

The atomic elements in specific combinations come together under specific conditions to form innumerable structures of various kinds, only to disintegrate after a specific interval of time or under specific environments into their component atoms to be recycled to form new structures of similar or dissimilar kinds. Recycling of these basic atomic material units is therefore the fundamental law and characteristic of the material world in nature. Living organisms are often described as lumps of conscious matter. It remains to be seen if, besides their constituent material contents, souls of all living organisms also form an integral part of the recycling nature. Modern science, so far, has no answers, and even if there are answers, the question is only open to debate without freedom from bondages of religious dogmatisms, prejudices, and blind beliefs in our religious metanarratives. Moreover, just because something is scientifically difficult to prove for the time being does not make it impossible. We are aware of the history, that even celebrated scientists as Lord Kelvin and A.A. Michelson, by the end of the nineteenth century, had emphatically declared, 'all that was to be discovered has already been done so, and no further developments in physical science is possible'. And yet, the spectacular discoveries of radioactivity, X-rays, electrons, protons, neutrons, relativity, uncertainty principle, de Broglie hypothesis and wave-particle duality, planetary model for atom, concepts of electron jumps into higher electron orbits around central nucleus of atoms, multi-universes (multiverse), and quantum physics have pushed the frontiers of knowledge beyond imagination and perception of even the most celebrated scientists of the nineteenth century mentioned above. However, consciousness is essential for any understanding and comprehension. Material creation, its beauty and grandeur, has no value without the presence of a conscious observer. Consciousness is therefore at the centre of all creation and the universe is essentially biocentric and not material-centric, as is generally believed. Today, new thinking, interpretations, and paradigm shifts on related concepts as possible explanations are emerging in the form of 'theory of morphic or morphogenetic fields, morphic resonance and morphogenesis' proposed and pioneered by Rupert Sheldrake, 'theory of epigenetics' by Bruce H. Lipton, and 'theory of biocentrism' proposed by Robert Lanza. Sir William Lawrence Bragg (NL) had once very rightly said: 'The important thing in science is not so much to obtain new facts as to discover new ways of thinking about them, because the sole purpose and aim of science is to do honour to the human spirit'.

1.6 Observed and Reported Cases of Reincarnation/Rebirth/Life after Death

Considerable data has now been gathered on modern scientific logic, experimental analysis, and voluminous amount of observations and experiences collected from thousands of cases of rebirth of individuals, cutting across continents, nationalities, cultures, religious faiths, and physical conditions of existence on the earth. All these studies, rigorously tested on the strength of statistical and regression analysis as reported, are suggesting the possibility of a common cause, purpose, process, reason, and science for our repeated cyclic births, spanning over several centuries and irregular time intervals between each birth. There is apparently a common denominator in observations recorded by these individuals of the case studies about experiences felt and memorized between earlier lives and rebirth. Therefore, whether we understand or do not understand, willingly accept or unwillingly ignore, consciously subscribe to or thoughtlessly discard, we must be magnanimously open to accept the fact as the scientific truth and not obstinately refuse with a preconditioned mindset that there has to be but one universal common theory or law which govern the existence of the entire human race and other living beings on earth, and for cycles of continued existence through births and rebirths. If, in case, we assume that some form of soul persists beyond death, it remains to be explained what particle is that soul made of, what kind and nature of known or unknown forces holds it together, and how does it interact with ordinary matter. Unfortunately, no supporters of life after death has tried to do the hard work of explaining how the basic physics of atoms and electrons beyond rules laid down by the Standard Model of Particle Physics would have to be altered or interpreted in order to explain this. Continued belief in life after death either requires entirely new physics and understanding on how that interacts with the familiar matter, or an entirely new but innovative explanation and interpretation on the basis of the existing laws of physics. We need to arrive at some satisfactory scientific explanation than to remain perpetually ignorant and clouded in blind faith and orthodoxy. Most importantly, we need to understand that our belief in rebirth of an individual from the historical past is factually linked only to comparative similarities of the qualities of head, heart, valour, and wits with someone born in the present. We seldom bother, compare, or consider their physical body structure, constitution, or appearances. This essentially conveys the scientific message that it is not the physical return in rebirth of an individual from the past, but the characteristics and power of the self-replicating DNA molecule within cellular replication processes in shaping the birth of a new individual with nearly similar or identical attributes in association with epigenetic environment during conception, gestation development, and birth. We, therefore, only need to seek a convincing scientific explanation for transfer of memory and information from one generation to the other than to pursue the impossible reality of rebirth after death. It is, in fact, a purely accidental, near-exact resemblance of an individual in qualities of head, heart, mind, thoughts, and deeds with someone who had lived in the historical past and whose memories are preserved in our documentary records that prompts us to believe in his/her cyclic rebirth. In the absence of memory or such documented record about any person who had lived in the past, belief in rebirth loses all its consideration, relevance, and significance. Moharir has very strongly argued against the possibility of the concept of rebirth. However, the only scientifically justifiable truth is the possible birth of a new individual resembling in characteristics with someone who had displayed similar traits in the past. Such individual characteristic traits are repeatedly reproduced in human beings over specific intervals of time from specific combinations and interaction of self-replicating genes (DNA) during cellular replication processes and cyclic environmental conditions (terrestrial and cosmic both inclusive). Therefore, physical return in rebirth of individuals after death is just not possible. It is only the repeat cyclic emergence of the characteristic traits and attributes in new individuals arising from the routine manifestation of the self-replicating DNA molecules and combination of millions of encoded proteins synthesized by them in response to the stimulus from the surrounding environment.

Renowned biologist Professor Richard Dawkins also mentions in his renowned book *The Selfish Gene*, and it is worth quoting here: 'Individuals are not stable things, they are fleeting. Chromosomes (genes) too are shuffled into oblivion, like hands of cards soon after they are dealt. But the cards themselves survive the shuffling. The cards are the genes. The genes are not destroyed by crossing over in shuffling them, they merely change partners and march on. Of course they march on. That is their business. They are the replicators and we are their survival machines. When we have served our purpose we are cast aside. But the genes are denizens of geological time: Genes are forever.' 'For more than three thousand million years, DNA has been the only replicator worth talking about in the world. But this does not necessarily hold these monopoly rights for all time. Whenever conditions arise in which a new kind of replicator can make copies of itself, the new replicators will tend to takeover, and start a new kind of evolution of their own.'

1.7 Vedic Philosophy about Birth, Death, and Reincarnation/Rebirth

The earliest references to the concept and practical truth about birth, death, and rebirth in human beings comes from the Vedic scriptures and Vedic civilization that flourished in ancient India about 25,000 years ago. The first entry and final exit of what is called the 'prana' or the 'soul' from the body were synonymous with life and death. The Indian concepts of breath and energy, prana, have predated and indeed inspired those originating from Europe and China. Hindus believe that in addition to the physical body, there is an astral body connected to the physical body by means of a thread, which is severed at death. The civilization at Vedic times was homogenously apolitical and not divided between multitude of religious groups, factions, and faiths, as it is now in the twenty-first century. The emphatic statement on the truth about rebirth is found in the words of Shri Krishna, delivered on the battlefield of Kurukshetra on 16 October 5561 BC (*date corresponding to the Indian calendar system that is prevalent, practised, and recorded in verses in the Shrimad Bhagavadgita and interpolated back in Gregorian calendar for easy comprehension of the elapsed time span by Dr P.V. Vartak*). Here, Shri Krishna clearly states about hundreds of death and rebirth cycles of everyone present in the battlefield with the only difference that while everyone else has forgotten about their repeated past lives between their deaths and rebirths, Shri Krishna distinctly remembers his own. Thousands of years after Shri Krishna, it was

Gautama Buddha who has been known to have remembered all his past births and deaths, which include 357 lives as human beings, 66 as gods, and 123 as animals, indicating thereby the factual possibility of transmigration of soul from human to 'godly angelic' individuals to animal life forms between successive births. Surprisingly however, there is neither the mention nor the description of the sequential order of the births and rebirths of Gautama Buddha. In both these cases, it is impossible to believe that both Shri Krishna and Gautama Buddha should have factually remembered their individual identity through all the cycles of their births, deaths, and rebirths. It seems more probable, reasonable, logical, and scientifically consistent to believe that both Shri Krishna and Gautama Buddha, being knowledgeable about Vedic philosophy and Upanishads (Buddhism as a religion was not even born until Buddha lived his life), were, in fact, citing their own lives, deaths, and rebirths as metaphoric examples in explaining the cardinal principle of perpetually cyclic nature of material creation, existence, and destruction going on in the universe, and perhaps not of the individuals or their enigmatic souls. This cycle is common to both the inanimate and animate matter and nothing more. It is perhaps our enamoured love, affection, appreciation, and emotional attachment to the personalities, qualities, and teachings of both Shri Krishna and Gautama Buddha individually that have blinded us to overlook the factual scientific truth in their statements and mistakenly assume them to being endowed with supernatural powers. Both Shri Krishna and Gautama Buddha were human beings like any other individual. Shri Krishna was bestowed and invoked with godhood more than 2,500 years after his death, as per records mentioned by Dr P.V. Vartak, and Gautama Buddha, during his own lifetime, had clearly emphasized that he was neither a God nor a messenger of a God. His enlightenment was not the result of a supernatural prowess, power, process, or agency, but rather the result of close and minute attention he paid to the nature of the human mind, which could be rediscovered by anyone. On the contrary, Buddhism, long after Buddha was gone, denies the concept of an eternal, individualized soul, but does include some ideas resembling the soul such as *skanda*s, which carry memories of a person's karma into future lives, and an advanced practitioner of Buddhism can attain the 'rainbow body', which enables one to exist beyond the physical body.

1.8 Religious Philosophies Based on Third-Person Accounts

It is a historical fact that stories about the life, work, and philosophy of both Shri Krishna and Gautama Buddha and also of Jesus Christ, Prophet Muhammad, Lord Mahavir, and Guru Nanak were written, compiled, edited, or interpreted by their followers long after they were gone. Neither of them had told nor even written their biographies. Information about all of them has descended down to us from the records written by third persons, either contemporary or otherwise. The *Mahabharata* itself has seen three editions before coming into the present form, originally containing 8,800 verses written by Ved Vyasa to 24,000 verses in the version edited by Rishi Vaishampayan, and finally to 100,000 verses in the version compiled and edited by Rishi Sauti, sequentially within a span of about 1,000 years from Ved Vyasa. Therefore, there appears to be something fundamentally wrong or quite possibly a distortion in communication and in understanding the messages of both Shri Krishna and Gautama Buddha about the factual reality or mystery of remembering their own births and rebirths. Even in the case of Shri Ram in the epic *Ramayana*, he has been essentially described as an ordinary human being all through the text, except a brief mention to his (Ram's) being an incarnation in the 'Bal-Kaand' and 'Sunder-Kaand' chapters.

The very fact that the psychic, intuitive, spiritual, or telepathic communication over long distances can be established with even pet or wild animals by animal communicators today suggests that there exists a common, subtle bond between all life forms, because consciousness within plants, human beings, and all other forms of animate life forms is incredibly similar[6]. Both Shri Krishna and Gautama Buddha clearly stand out as the only human beings who understood the true nature of the cyclic universe. No wonder, they both are considered by the Hindus as the reincarnations of Lord Vishnu, the omnipresent, potential cosmic consciousness or the force of nature that sustains and recycles material creation. Therefore, there appears to be some justification for a thorough scientific investigation about why should memory about past births, even in a very few reported cases, could be retained, whereas in majority of other individuals gets totally absent or lost.

1.9 Modern Concept of Atoms and Molecules: Their Structures, Combinations, and Functions

The earliest references to the concepts of atoms and molecules can be found in the *Mahabharata* (5561 BC) with the mention of the use of atomic weapon-like devices called *Bramhastra* in this war. The factual description of the situation that arose after the detonation of Bramhastra corresponds parallel to the description recorded in the modern history after the first two atomic nuclear fission bombs were dropped on the cities of Hiroshima and Nagasaki in Japan during World War II. There is no description about how the sages and rishis of the Vedic times arrived at the concepts of atom and molecules described in Sanskrit as *anuu* and *parmanuu* respectively, but they were certainly aware of this reality. They even widely using the atomic or molecular processes of electroplating for depositing silver and gold over base metals. Science, technology, and industry were indeed a part of the Vedic culture.

6 Daniel Chamovitz and Rupert Sheldrake, *Dogs That Know When Their Owners Are Coming Home: And Other Unexplained Powers of Animals* (New York: Three River Press, 2011).

The idea of atoms constituting the material world originated in antiquity. Leucippus and Epicurus, the Greek philosophers, were already talking about matter being born from infinity which consisted of endless small particles in eternal motion. Democritus Abdera, another Greek philosopher (about 500 BC), wrote in an eloquent statement on atomic hypothesis: 'By convention sour, by convention sweet, by convention coloured; in reality, nothing but atoms and the void'. It was the great English chemist John Dalton who not only reiterated the atomic concept in 1808, but also showed that atoms of dissimilar elements combine in some fixed proportions. The atoms (of about 118 kinds) of similar or dissimilar elements present in nature in combinations enter into the composition of known composite substances. The atoms or molecules can only vibrate without displacement like the stems of wheat or maize crop plants, which sways in the wind but without changing their places. Further, developments in the modern theory of atomic structure of matter had made it very clear that the size of the atoms, if they existed, would be extremely small to be perceived directly by our senses or even seen under the most powerful microscope. To confirm the physical reality of the existence of atoms, an ingenious idea was adopted to assume or theorize that atoms indeed existed and then develop some logical experiments based on this assumption in anticipation of some perceptible consequences. Any matching of observed consequences in accordance with assumptions would mean an indirect confirmation for the existence of atoms. Several experiments conducted by Bernoulli, James Clerk Maxwell, Ludwig Boltzmann, Robert Boyle, Jacques Cesar Charles, and finally Albert Einstein unequivocally demonstrated that atoms indeed exist. Robert Brown demonstrated and recognized the perpetual motion of pollen grains suspended in water; the Brownian motion to be caused by the pushing thrusts exerted on the pollen grains by continually dynamic molecules of water made of two hydrogen atoms joined together to one oxygen atom. Albert Einstein developed a mathematical theory to explain the Brownian motion whose theoretical predictions were not only confirmed by Jean Baptiste Perrin, but even the size of atoms were calculated by him to be of the order of a billionth part of a metre in diameter. It was however left to Sir J.J. Thomson, Ernest Rutherford, Niels Bohr, and several others to fully describe how an atom looks like and how it functions. Perhaps, the best possible examples of the power of formulation of logical conceptual theories are the law of periodic table of elements discovered by Dmitri I. Mendeleev, who predicted the existence and properties of new elements long before they were physically discovered in nature. More recently, the theoretical prediction of the existence of an elementary particle, 'The Higgs Boson', also nicknamed as 'The God Particle', that provides mass to energy was invented by Peter Higgs almost 50 years before it was experimentally discovered at the CERN (European Centre for Nuclear Research, Geneva) in 2012–13. The mechanisms involved in these theoretical models do not make it a precondition to physically experience observations with our five senses before we understand and accept them, as has been imprinted in our minds by the classical Newtonian physics. For example, look at the new concept of an electron jumping instantaneously from one orbit shell around the nucleus to another without physically moving across the space between the consecutive shells. Here, electrons just disappear from one orbit shell and reappear in the other. This disappearance and reappearance of electron is akin to its death in one orbit shell and rebirth in the other; alternately, disappearing from one universe and reappearing into another. Mechanisms and explanations of such phenomena are not only beyond our imagination, but can only be explained on the basis of quantum mechanics and not by classical physics. Whereas classical Newtonian physics stood for absolute physical quantities and their absolute measurements, modern physics believes in the impossibility of absolute quantities and their measurements, which are not only relative but represent only the probabilities of their being a reality.

1.10 Quanta and Quantum Particles

The discovery of atom (irrespective of its 118 different elemental kinds) marks the landmark departure from the classical physical science. Atoms consist of over 99.9 per cent empty space with over 99.9 per cent of their masses being concentrated within a minute region at the centre called the nucleus, as compared to the size of the atoms. The nuclei of atoms were discovered to be charged electrically positive, and nuclear physicists pictured the atom as a miniature solar system with distribution of negatively charged electrons around the nucleus to make the atom electrically neutral. This theoretical picture defied the classical Newtonian laws of motion and new laws had to be discovered to explain the perpetual motion of electrons without losing their energy and spirally colliding into the nucleus, leading to its annihilation or something to that effect. Nothing like this happens in reality and to explain the motion of electrons around the nuclei of atoms, Niels Bohr adopted the concept described by Max Planck. He explained that a body absorbs or emits energy in the form of radiation, not continuously but discontinuously in integral multiples of definite amount of packets called quantum. The magnitude of the quantum depends on the vibration frequency of the oscillator, that is, electron. If v is the frequency of vibration, the quantum Q of energy is given by $Q = ℏ.v$, where $ℏ$ is Planck's universal constant. Energy can be taken up or given out in such quanta only. The role of electrons is primordial in that it is the electron which gives a substance most of its physical and chemical properties, and it is its number which determines the physical identity of the elemental atom, that is, whether it is hydrogen, iron, or uranium. Chemical combinations are always brought about when electrons are shared or exchanged between two or more interacting atoms to form structures. Both atoms and molecules (depending on the number of atoms involved in combination to form a molecule) constitute quantum particles in perpetual state of vibration with characteristic frequencies and wavelengths. The diameters of the atoms are of the order of a ten millionth of a millimetre, and that of the least voluminous molecules measure two to three times as much. The individual molecules routinely encountered in organic (or biological chemistry) assume much larger sizes and can be easily visualized under powerful electron or atomic force microscopes. In molecules of similar and dissimilar atoms, regions of varying electron density are usually found around atoms and their bonds. The electron density distribution is therefore a measure of the probability of an electron being present at a specific location along the molecular length. A look at the electron density map or the structural formula of a molecule is enough to suggest to a chemist, which regions are electron-rich and vulnerable to electrophilic attack, and which are more likely to attract nucleophilic reagents, thereby permitting calculation of the external electrostatic potential and the interactive energy between molecules or between parts of the same molecule. The three great themes which emerged in the twentieth century, namely the atom, the computer, and the gene have revolutionized science and changed the human mindset. Further, Werner Heisenberg's uncertainty principle, Albert Einstein's theory of relativity, and Erwin Schrodinger's wave mechanics (Quantum Mechanics) laid the foundations of quantum physics and elucidation of the structure and function of the DNA (gene) by James D. Watson and that of the molecular biology by F.H.C. Crick.

1.11 What Is Life?

'Functional emergence with evolution' and vitalism are the two mainstream concepts which have dominated scientific thoughts about characterization and nature of all living systems. While functionalism characterizes life by its self-organizational and self-replicating arrangements leading to purposeful functions and behaviour, the proponents of 'artificial life' also consider many non-biological systems such as self-organizing computer programs with lifelike functions to be alive. If the flow of controlled amount of quantized electric charge on electrons in the form of a sequential computer program can replicate lifelike functions and behaviour, why cannot the actual flow of electric charge through body systems (which are essentially electrical in nature mediated by the flow of atomic ions) of all living organisms and their control over the operational function and behaviour of the organisms be primarily attributed to electric charge rather than to the hypothetical, abstract, illusive, and enigmatic concept of the soul? Electricity is both a fundamental and universal natural entity. It consists of positive and negatively charged particles that mutually exhibit attractions and repulsions. Such attractions and repulsions manifest themselves into the movement of these charged particles to setup and establish flow of electric currents. This form of energy plays a critical role in the proper function of the metabolism of our body and its organs. Electrical activity in our body is initiated by the ions and their movements through millions of ion channels. An ion is an atom or a group of atoms (molecules) carrying an electric charge by virtue of having gained or lost one or more valence electrons. Valence electrons are those that move in the outermost ring of electrons orbiting around the nuclei of the atoms. Ions may exist in solid, liquid, or gaseous environments. Ionic solid chemical compounds are generally known as **salts**, and the ions existing in liquid state as the **electrolytes**. Electrolytes in solutions conduct electric currents and are decomposed by electric currents. The process of such decomposition of electrolytes in solutions is known as **electrolysis**. Electrolytes play an essential role in the functioning of our bodies. Cells create electrical energy when ions move from within the cells to solutions outside the cell membranes. Ions, as we understand, play an important role in the bodies of all living organisms. Calcium, potassium, sodium, chloride, oxygen, carbon, hydrogen, nitrogen, and copper are some of the key ions that participate in the body's electrical events. Potassium is the major positive ion inside the cell. Sodium is the major positive ion found in the fluid outside the cell. Oxygen as a gas is essential for the production of cellular energy. Carbon forms the main component of all organic molecules such as carbohydrates, lipids, proteins, and nucleic acids. Hydrogen in its ionic form is influential in controlling the pH (acidity and alkalinity) of all body fluids. Nitrogen is an important structural component of all genetic material (nucleic acids). Calcium, the major component of bones and teeth in its ionic form, is essential in muscle contraction, impulse conduction in nerves, and blood clotting. Phosphorous in association with calcium contributes to the bone crystalline matrix structure and is an essential component of nucleic acids and ATP molecules. Potassium in its ionic form is the major positive (cation) ion, necessary for conduction of nerve impulses and muscle contraction. Likewise, ions of sulphur, chlorine, magnesium, iodine, iron, chromium, cobalt, fluorine, manganese, molybdenum, selenium, vanadium, and zinc have very specific roles to play in body metabolic activities, metabolisms, and its healthy functioning[7]. Thus, all our body activities such as thinking, emotional responses, eating, listening, speaking, muscular movements, glandular secretions, digestion, excretions, temperature regulation, and every bodily action is performed as a result of the movement of ions or electrically charged molecules. These little known but crucially important movements of ionic biomolecules (proteins) found in every cell of our body and in living organisms on earth regulate the lives of all bio-organisms from the moment of conception to their last breath. Ion channels

7 See 'Ions: The Body's Electrical Energy Source' by Mark T. Nielsen, Professor, Department of Biology, University of Utah, Research Article in Trace Minerals Research, 2015.

are truly the 'spark of life', for they govern every aspect of our life and behaviour. From the lashing of the sperm's tail to sexual attraction, the beating of our hearts, the craving for coffee, ice cream or chocolate, and the feel of the warmth from sun on our skin—everything is underpinned by ion-channel activity. The case of the Venus flytrap plant (Pitcher plant) which feels the presence of its prey is very similar to the way we feel a fly crawling on our body. Touch receptors in our skin sense the insect and activate an electrical signal that pass along our sensory nerves to the brain. The brain registers the signal and interprets the presence of the fly and stimulates reaction through muscular responses. Similarly, when the insect rubs against the hairs of the Venus flytrap, it induces an electrical signal that radiates throughout the leaves. As a result, the ion channels in the leaf cell membrane get suddenly activated to shut the flytrap in less than one-tenth of a second to catch the insect as its prey. Thus, ions play an important role in the bodies of all living organisms. Calcium, potassium, sodium, chloride, and copper ions participate in the body's electrical events. Potassium is the major positive ion inside the cells, and sodium in the fluids outside the cells. Ionic chloride is the most abundant negative ion. Any imbalance of these ions in the bodies of organisms or inhibition of sodium ion transport across cell membranes leads to dysfunction in the conduction of electrical messages. Such dysfunction produces disturbances and the loss of ability to maintain stable internal conditions. No wonder, an impaired functioning of ion channels is responsible for many human, plant, and animal diseases. Ion channels are the gatekeepers of the cells, and their opening and closing is controlled by intracellular and extracellular chemicals, mechanical stress, or changes in the voltage difference across cell membranes. Farm animals such as pigs that suddenly shiver themselves to death, a herd of goats that falls over when suddenly startled or threatened, people with cystic fibrosis, epilepsy, heart arrhythmias and migraine—all are the victims of a factual dysfunction of their ion channels. Historically, work done by some of the greatest researchers such as Alesandro Volta, Humphry Davy, Michael Faraday, Andre-Marie Ampere, James Clerk Maxwell, and several others conclusively demonstrated that there is essentially no difference between bioenergy and electricity that runs through voltaic pile, with further realization and conviction that psychic or bioenergy activities and all aspects of body metabolisms from the functioning of various glands, organs, brain, and heart arise from the electrical activity of over thirty billion cells in human body. Not only this, electricity is also the power behind all our senses and emotions. Bioenergy is indeed real and a physically based phenomenon.

Dick Frans Swaab, an internationally acclaimed researcher on human brain, clearly mentions in his book *We are our Brains: From the Womb to Alzheimer's*: 'I have yet to hear a good argument against my simple conclusion that the "mind" is the product of the activity of our hundred billion brain cells and the "soul" merely a misconception. The universality of the notion of a "soul" seems merely to spring from mankind's fear of death, the longing to see the dear departed once again, and the misplaced, arrogant idea that we are so important that something must remain of us after death. The product of the interaction of all these billions of neuron cells is what we call "mind". Just as kidneys produce urine, the brain produces mind, as Jacob Moleschott (1882–1893) so immutably put it. But now we know what this process actually entails; electrical activity, the release of chemical messengers, changes in cell contacts and alterations in the activity of nerve cells. Brain scans are used not only to trace diseases of the brain but also to show which areas light up during different activities, so that we know which parts we use to read, think, calculate, listen to music, have religious experiences, fall in love, or become sexually excited. By observing the changing patterns of the brain, we can train it to function differently. Malfunction in this efficient information processing machine cause psychiatric and neurological disorders. Paradoxically, these disorders tell us much more about the way in which the brain normally functions.' As humans are all genetically different, so is the electrical system of every human body. Each person has his specific electrical fingerprint that defines their body electrical structure. Some people are genetically predisposed with additional high levels of current than most other people. No wonder, a touch by hand of an appropriately electrically charged individual may be enough to bridge the disrupted electric current flow in the body of a physically injured person.

Perhaps, in a way, we may be failing to recognize electric charge to be the de facto soul, which is considered and held responsible for the function and behaviour of all living organisms. It is pertinent to reason, argue, and ponder whether our ancient concept of soul may, in fact, be a religious dogma or a prejudiced obsession descended down to us through thousands of years of human civilizations. Has this dogmatic concept by any chance prevented us from thinking objectively and taking a truly scientific look at the 'soul' beyond reasons already discussed above?

The term 'emergence' implies a hierarchical organization, built from simple components at lower levels with life arising from complex interactions within and between the constituent component parts. Life, therefore, is believed to emerge from complex interactions between atoms, ions, and polar or non-polar biomolecules made up of atoms. The biomolecules on the other hand are more complex and complicated. Their organization into structures of biological systems, interactions, properties, functions, and behaviour are governed by the nature, position, and properties of various types of atoms or group of atoms and their movements within and across biological systems, mediated through the specific and specialized ion channels. Such functional and emergent approaches, based on reductionism, are being frequently used these days in molecular biology. On the other hand, vitalism, the other mainstream, based on electromagnetism or essentially on imaginary forces from outside the familiar realm of science, stands discarded for good with the advent of quantum mechanics. Erwin Schrodinger, the founder of quantum mechanics, suggested in 1944 that the essential framework of life is engrained in 'aperiodic lattices', and all living systems are fundamentally quantized. This description is relevant for both DNA and ribonucleic acid (RNA), the cytoskeletal protein assemblies, microtubules, and actin gels that criss-cross the entire cell matrix. With recent evidence of biomolecules being also capable of harnessing ambient heat and energy to promote their functional quantum states instead of causing discoherence, the non-local quantum correlations amongst the biomolecules are considered to be responsible for unified inherent behaviours of living systems (Roger Penrose). It is a general opinion of all celebrated scientists since the time of Erwin Schrodinger that life is related to organized quantum processes in π electron resonance clouds within biomolecules. Biology perhaps evolved initially from simple oil-water interfaces and adopted to utilize cooperative quantum processes to its best advantage with minimum expenditure of energy.

Three theories are currently in vogue regarding the origin of life. One assumes an involvement of a 'creator', the second involves a sudden spontaneous chemical activity leading to formation of self-replicating biomolecules, and the third assumes seeding of the earth from extraterrestrial (exobiology) sources such as meteorites, comets, and asteroids. However, such explanations still need to explain the origin of life in conditions of extraterrestrial space before transportation to earth for manifestation and proliferation. Further, biomolecules such as simple peptides, sugars, lipids, and nucleic acids have been observed to form spontaneously in marine saltwater or near geothermal vents (geysers), volcanoes, and in clay minerals. What seems mysterious though is their incorporation, culmination, evolution, and adaptation into structural organelles and their coalescence to become the cooperating parts of an integrated biological cell as the basic units of all life forms, irrespective of their origin from soil, plant, animal, or aquatic source. All these appear to suggest 'intelligent design' and obviously 'creationism'. But according to Roger Penrose, intelligent design simply reflects the type of Platonic (harmless or ineffectual) information embedded in the Planck scale. If this is true, it implies that all living systems are perpetually in touch with some deeper reality of the universe through quantum states. Even Swami Satyananda Saraswati observes that 'research on the nature of available energies in the universe indicate that consciousness may be independent from the body of organisms, suggesting thereby, that all living organisms may be integrally connected to the universal consciousness'. Such a conclusion has also been advanced earlier in this book during discussion on supersymmetry. However, this does not mean that all quantum information devices must also be 'alive'. Only organic molecules and cytoskeletal protein lattices may be endowed with inherent flexibility to harness ambient energy for quantum coherent states to interact and adjust with the Planck scale through quantum gravity processes and use photons as phase-ordered matter. But, since all animate and inanimate material world is built from atoms, the above argument implies that what we call 'conscious life' may be a special property endowed to only restricted atoms such as carbon, hydrogen (proton), nitrogen, calcium, sodium, sulphur, magnesium, phosphorus, potassium, and chlorine, and to molecules built from a combination of these atoms. These are the only few elements, particularly carbon, sodium, potassium, and hydrogen that uniformly and predominantly go into the structural make-up and in the functional operation of various body organs of all living organisms from soil, land, plant, insect, bird, or of aquatic origin, and each one working under command (or regulated by) of its conscious enigmatic entity called the soul. Just as a house under construction does not spontaneously emerge from a pile of bricks, similarly there is nothing conscious about an electron required to emerge as consciousness from a pile of atoms put together. Most of the piles of atoms do not produce anything. They process no information and do not generate any output. Still, however, some configurations of atoms indeed process information and generate output and are labelled as 'conscious'. And yet, it does not qualify as an emergent property as the house that emerges from bricks, the basic building block for a house. This appears to set consciousness apart from electric charge on electron, proton, or atomic ions. While a quantum of electric charge can be measured, a quantum of consciousness cannot be assayed so. Alternately, a certain amount of electric charge can always be expressed as a multiple of the quantum of charge on an electron, but consciousness cannot be similarly divided down to the level of an electron. This is because whereas electric charge is a physical quantity, consciousness is merely an attribute, a property that arises as a result of the combinations and permutations of connecting various building blocks from a huge 'body organism' space. It is an arbitrary definition and an arbitrary attribute of a specific association and group of atoms. It would therefore be worthwhile to examine from such a specific angle, the composition and sequential arrangement of atoms in adenine, thymine, cytosine, and guanine (A, T, C, and G) groups of molecules that makes up the composition of the DNA, program the syntheses of proteins, and initiate and sustain metabolism and functional activities of various organs at free will to generate what is called 'consciousness'.

1.12 What Is Soul?

The soul, since antiquity, has been associated with consciousness and freedom of all life forms that exist on earth. All religions that have flourished and perished and those still existing on earth have propounded notions of the soul. Soul and body together form one unique combination of nature. Everyone speaks about the soul, but rarely has anyone attempted to dare, ponder, or describe what exactly it is and what is its structure and configuration based on modern scientific origin. Despite tremendous developments in science and technology and increased resolving power of our instrumental detection techniques, soul, as a hidden illusive entity, continues to remain the most profound enigma of our life. Our knowledge about soul continues to be vague and, yet, we blindly admit that our soul identifies who we are. Each and every soul is believed to be an individual and an immortal entity created by nature. It is still not clear if it is the will of the soul that propels a body from birth to the end of its life, or is it the capacity and limitation of the developed body system that restricts the 'resident time' for the soul within itself? However, experience suggests that when a body system gets incapacitated (short circuited) to maintain the flow of electric charge to every body organ in a holistic way, the immortal soul exits it. This is why naturally debilitated bodies kept on external life support remain conscious and alive to some extent as long as the external support is continued. In a spectacular incident reported in the newspapers recently, a premature but healthy baby was delivered by a 15-week pregnant brain-dead mother, who suffered a stroke and had been maintained on life support system by the doctors in Budapest in Hungary to save the life of her baby. The baby was born alive and healthy through a caesarean operation at 27-week maturity and weighed 1.4 kg. It is very clear from this example that the brain of the mother had nothing to do with the development of the foetus, and the baby was either developing independently and guided by its own soul or by the soul of its mother, which did not reside in her brain but elsewhere. The external life support system merely helped in keeping the ion channels in the bodies of both the mother and developing foetus active.

A majority of people, in general, think of the soul to be a blob of immaterial spirit energy that persists after death, and that this sort of substance resides near our brain but drives around our body. The only entity that actually moves around our entire body system, consisting of billions of individual cells constituting various organs, is the electric charge and current. Vedas and Upanishads describe the soul to be residing in the heart of the human body. This seems to be logical in that it is indeed the heart that continually distributes and circulates oxygen, the principal currency for exchange of electric charge and generator of active ion channels in the body. This is a function analogous and similar to that of artificial life support systems. The purpose of both is to supply oxygen to the body through lungs. Any limitations in the supply of oxygen lead to insufficient generation of ions, and consequently, to feeble ionic currents to maintain all organs of multicellular body optimally functional. Here again, it is the essential role of electric charge that is underlined in generating consciousness. But what is the thing which not only generates but perpetually sustains the electric charge itself? Halit Eroglu, in his recent book, *The Theory of Everything*, an English translation of the revised and expanded third edition of the work *Die Weltformel-Die Urkraft des Universums* (e-Book, www.hc10.ed), maintains that the universe consists of simple components. An analogue clock also consists of simple components such as gears, screws, etc. It is only the interaction of these basic components according to a specific system that brings the clock to a running state. In the universe too, it is the interaction of individual components that make the 'clockwork' universe running. The space in the universe, as also the vacuum in its smallest dimensions, according to Eroglu, consists of unified and densely interconnected spheres with a strictly periodic structure called the 'spaceballs'. The spaceballs are magnetic monopoles and their elementary energy force manifests itself in the form of attraction to pull each other.

All physical phenomena are the consequences of the primal magnetism in the magnetic monopoles, the spaceballs. The electric charge, mass, and the basic components of matter, the atoms, stars, etc. arise from the interactions between these spaceballs, according to the following scheme:

(SpaceBall) Magnetism > Charge > Mass > Particles > Atoms > Stars

Magnetism causes emergence of electric charges and these generate mass, which then form particles that accumulate into atoms, and the atoms, in turn, produce all macroscopic bodies and celestial objects in the universe.

Magnetism in spaceballs is a hidden power which forms the elemental force in the universe and the entire universe is built-up electromagnetically. Therefore, electrodynamics and electromagnetic interactions have their origin in the quantized magnetism. The effects of the elemental magnetism become apparent from the transport of charge. According to Eroglu, magnetism is the cause of electrodynamics and it brings out the charges as an effect and not the other way round. Physical calculations do not change by this order, but provide better understanding of the universe with different perspectives and new insights. The simplest electric charge is a point particle according to classical electromagnetic theory, for which the electric field is visualized as lines of force radiating out from the centre. Two opposite point charges, positive and negative, constitute an electric dipole. So we can call a point charge as an electric monopole. If we take an electric dipole and pull the charges separate, we get two electric monopoles. A bar magnet is an ancient example of magnetic dipole, with a north and a south pole. But when a bar magnet is cut into two halves, we do not get magnetic monopoles but two separate dipoles. The absence of magnetic monopoles is the only difference between electricity and magnetism, and magnetic monopoles have been accepted to be consistent with quantum mechanics and restore the symmetry between electricity and magnetism. So far, magnetic monopoles have not been detected, and it is not possible to directly observe them because they themselves show no observable physical events. All physical events actually emerge from the interactions of dipoles, which are formed by external influences. Halit Eroglu's explanation appears to be consistent with the discussion developed in this paper. It therefore appears to suggest that physics and physical laws concerning creation, accumulation, and interaction of magnetic monopoles in the space vacuum has something to do with the origin or the identity of what we call the soul. Since magnetic monopoles represent the elementary, primordial, all-pervading form of energy in the universe from which every other matter is created, it connects well as the common thread with the origin and function of all living creatures on the earth. Whatever may be the truth, the questions that still remain unanswered are: What form does the soul energy take? What is its ultimate origin, constitution, nature, and location inside the body of the organism and how does it interact with other ordinary atoms? It is also not clearly known whether it is the same individual soul that takes residence within the body from the moment of birth/ conception to death with its known identity of 'self' or 'me'. If it is the same soul that remains resident in the body from birth till death, then how does it lose its identity, for example, when ridden with Alzheimer's disease? Does the root cause for Alzheimer's disease change the very identity of what we call the soul? Truly speaking, it is the people around us, and in family, or our parents, and the society in general who maintain and keep reminding us about our identity of being Mr X or Mr Y. Imagine a child born in the wild, who somehow survives alone after his birth, will ever know his identity except realizing that he is only a conscious creature. As all living creatures on earth remain continually connected to the oxygen reservoir of atmosphere from the moment of birth to the last breath, there is therefore a reason to believe that we (as an individual soul) continually remain in touch with universal consciousness (energy/force) from birth unto death, through a subtle, unknown mechanism ingrained within our body systems. The soul, taking a permanent residence within the body for a lifetime, appears to be a pleasant likeable myth. Here, the role of subtle electrical conduits, the millions of ion channels (in the language of modern biology) or the conduits (*Nadi*) identified and known since millenniums in India for circulation of consciousness in our bodies, known as *Ida*, *Pingala*, and *Sushumna*, and the power grids called the chakras for maintaining a continuous connection for functioning of various body organs under their control, besides regulating the flood of universal consciousness within cells and organs of body systems, appears to be very rational. The subtle energy of body is believed to have both physical and psychic properties and its most intense form is represented by the Vedic concept of serpent Kundalini, which normally remains dormant in each and every individual. This concept of continuous connection can be easily understood when I say: 'my house has running water for 24 hours'. Here, it does not mean that the same quantity of water stays in my house for 24 hours, but only that my house is connected to an unlimited source or a reservoir, knowing well that I am using different water every time I open the tap in my house. Still however, the statement also qualifies that water stays in my house for 24 hours. Similarly, consciousness also stays in our bodies through continual connection to its universal source from the moment of birth to the last breath. A quantum entity called the soul, taking a permanent residence in the body, therefore appears to be a very narrow and selfish interpretation and an antique deception.

1.13 Kundalini and Human Consciousness

Besides soul and rebirth, the other profound concepts from the Indian philosophy have been the kundalini and the chakras, which are believed to be deeply interconnected. Kundalini is known as the sleeping, dormant potential energy force in the human body that springs up from the root of the spinal cord. While in the male body, it is believed to be located in the perineum, between the urinary and excretory organs, in a female body its location is at the root of the uterus in the cervix. Both these locations within the male and female bodies are collectively called the *muladhar chakra*. This muladhar chakra is in fact a glandular physical structure. The energy force from the kundalini can be awakened through special yogic training and practises of asanas (postures), pranayama (breathing control), *kriya* (cleansing acts), and meditation (mind control/concentration of mind). Kundalini yoga is a tantric tradition, wherein the range of mental experience is broadened beyond the framework of time, space, and object, and tremendous energy is released within the body. Experiences, which have been subjectively described for thousands of years in the historical past by the names such as; nirvana, moksha, emancipation, self-realization, salvation, liberation, *buddhattva*, or samadhi without understanding them properly, are in fact related only to the awakening of kundalini and nothing else. And experiencing physical, mental, and psychic state within the human body described under such synonymous terminologies like nirvana, moksha, communion, union, *kaivalya*, liberation, emancipation, self-realization, and salvation, concerning the awakening of kundalini, has been the only goal of human spiritual life and of people spending their entire life in pursuit of spirituality. The ignorant man originally named kundalini energy after the gods, goddesses, angels, or divinities, and subsequently to the 'prana shakti'. Incidentally, references to the 'path of the initiates' and the 'stairway to the heavens' as described in The Bible, in fact factually refers to the awakening of the kundalini. The ascent of the kundalini and descent of the experienced spiritual grace that followed from it was symbolized as the cross by the Christians. The cross therefore symbolically represents the smooth flow of kundalini energy through the power grids called the chakras. The two holes on either side of human spinal cord in cross section are like conduits for all the sensory nerves to pass. These left and right conduits have been given the names as the ida and pingala nadis respectively. The ida and pingala represent the basic duality, masculine and feminine, or the logical and intuitive aspects of life, and are called Shiva and Shakti. Life is created based on this duality.

Everything is primordial before duality is created. The terms 'masculine' and 'feminine' do not represent the sex but certain natural qualities in nature, which have been identified to be characteristically masculine and such others as characteristically feminine. Therefore, it is the dominance of the ida or the pingala that determines the pronounced behaviour of any individual, irrespective of donning male or female bodies. Ida and pingala have been roughly translated to be respectively controlling the human mind and the body. They (nadis) do not exist in terms of any physical structures, but only in terms of a functional relationship of the prana energy. Vital life giving prana energy is attributed to the pingala and mind/*chitta* or consciousness to the ida. Pingala is also defined as the basic, dynamic, active, positive, psychosomatic, masculine, yang energy within human personality responsible for driving the sensory organs. On the contrary, ida is the passive, receptive, negative, and feminine yin energy that controls the sense organs and provides knowledge and awareness of the world around us.

It is our common knowledge that when two equal and opposite forces balance each other, a third force arises. Therefore, when prana energy, through ida and pingala, is balanced and trigger open the switch at the muladhar chakra, a third force called the sushumna arises. It is only when the sushumna/kundalini is aroused that the prana energy rises sequentially upward from the muladhar to the *sahasrasara* and provides a blissful experience of union with the universal cosmic consciousness. This is the state, according to Carl

Jung, of achieving and experiencing a stable, peaceful, divine, and dynamically prolonged bliss.

A majority of people live and die with their prana energy actively flowing only within ida and pingala nadis. Despite adequate flow of energy prana through ida and pingala and continued effective life possible for an individual, their central space, sushumna nadi, remains practically dormant. However, sushumna nadi, which is the most significant to human physiology and life, becomes active when prana energy flowing through ida and pingala enters it through the muladhara chakra. The muladhar merely acts as a switch for releasing the flow of kundalini, but its actual location rests in the sahasrasara chakra located in brain.

The seven chakras namely, *muladhar*, *swadhisthana*, *manipur*, *anahat*, *vishuddhi*, *adnya*, and *sahasrasara* individually exercise control over various organs of the human body, and for physically, physiologically, metabolically, mentally and psychologically healthful living. The flow of prana energy through all the seven chakras and three nadis, ida, pingala, and sushumna is required to be smooth. In case of any obstruction to its flow at or in between any chakra, the organs under control of that chakra indicate signs of stress or dysfunction, and ultimately succumb to disease or failure with serious consequences, if ignored for long.

1.14 Evidence for the Existence of Nadis and Chakras

The kundalini yoga is based on the premise that there exists a system of thousands and thousands of nadis/conduits spread across the matrix of human body. These nadis distribute mental, physical, and electrical energy throughout the body and are intimately linked to the nerves, neurons, blood vessels, and to various organs. There is no apparent structural system visible as nadis within the human body when dissected. Still however, yogis believe that nadis do exist and their pathways within bodies can be mapped. Nadis are dynamic, live, power conduits for the body and mind. Dr Hiroshi Motoyama, a renowned philosopher, psychologist, and parapsychologist from Japan is very emphatic about the reality of nadis and the chakras within the human body, based on the multiple experiments he has conducted. Dr Motoyama has demonstrated a positive correlation between any imbalance, malfunction of nadis, and emergence of symptoms of diseases in the body. Intuitively, the author of this book feels very strongly that the ancient concept of nadis is similar, akin, or identical to the existence of thousands of ion channels that transmit electrical charges and currents across molecules, cell membranes, and in biochemical metabolism within bodies of all conscious organisms, as a consequence of the movement and exchange of atomic, electrically charged ions. Discovery of the existence of ion channels is relatively recent, and their importance in understanding of human biology is advancing very rapidly.

Similarly, the painstaking experimental work done by Dr Hiroshi Motoyama and G.G. Hunt have established a positive correlation with the stimulation of individual chakras by the yoga practitioners, and corresponding physiological functional changes in the organs controlled by the respective chakras. Although, no physical or structural demarcation can be located for existence of the chakras within the human body, distinct functional characteristics corresponding to the familiar locations of the seven chakras have been discriminated. The traditional locations of the chakras, when activated by the yoga practitioners, have also been correlated with corresponding stimulation and vision of characteristic colours, emotions, and experiences. All these experiments certainly bring home the fact that the concept of chakras is based on sound parapsychological /physiological logic and reason. More than this, all phenomena concerning human body and its experiences involving ida, pingala and sushumna nadis, kundalini, prana, chakras, soul, mind and consciousness, biochemical metabolic or physical mechanisms, physiology, psychology, emotions, moods, grimaces, etc. are definitely related to the movement/transfer/

sharing of electric charges by means of atomic ions through thousands of ion channels within the bodies of conscious organisms.

1.15 What Is Death? How Does It Come About?

Death in a multicellular organism is never an instantaneous event, but is known to be a gradual closing down of the process in sequential stages. Brain cells die almost immediately, the heart follows next, then kidneys, the intestines, and in the end, skin and hair. Eyes retain their usefulness for six hours and must be removed within that period, if it is to be transplanted to some other individual. Muscles and nerve cells continue to retain their hold on the cells much longer after the death of the being, and therefore stand a chance for a possible revival with immediate electric shock treatment, and for later use for a cadaver organ transplant. Organ transplant is possible only because the energy that drives these organs is the same in all animal forms and the transplanted organs start deriving energy from the ion channels of the new body in which they are implanted. Avoiding possible rejection of the transplanted organ in a new body is only a matter of readjustment of the receptor proteins of the transplanted organ from the cadaver with those of the new body. The hydrogen protons/electric charges therefore gradually stop flowing through the body as a result of blockage or closure of its essential ion channels after death. In reality, death only marks the failure of the body system to maintain and regulate the flow of electric charges, mediated through circulation of oxygen in blood vessels and exchange of electric charges through and across cell membranes, neurons, muscles, and organs with the help of ions for a continued operation and functions. Oxygen infusion is often overlooked in regard to its role in ATP synthesis by establishing pathways that produce high-energy phosphate bonds. Natural degradation of cellular function is representative of a lack of oxygen and insufficient synthesis of ATP molecules, and ultimately the power of body cells. Soul represents a deeply felt moral and emotional attribute of a universal consciousness with the ability to induce or excite and exhibit expressions of kindness, love, affection, gratitude, sympathy, beauty, aesthetics, mood, art, music, anger, rage, hunger, and other subtle emotions as a result of the synthesis and secretion of specific hormones, enzymes, proteins, or other metabolites initiated or ignited by particular thought, nature of food consumed, ailment, or injury as demanded by the coherent body system, having a dynamic connection with the universal source of energy/consciousness. This is the reason why it is believed and actually experienced that souls of all life forms in the universe share a common inheritance, bond, identity, structure, nature, purpose, work, and destiny. No wonder, we feel tremendous affinity, love, affection, loyalty, concern, and complementary purpose for a collective cooperative existence on earth, and hold, although erroneously, our belief in transmigration of the soul through various life forms.

Hydrogen (proton/electron) therefore appears to stand appropriate for the identity of the common thread that connects the cosmic energy with the consciousness flowing through all the living organisms. Questionably, if this is possible, it is still a mystery that how hydrogen (proton) or, more precisely, the magnetic monopoles culminate and form a complex composite, a quasi-quantum particulate consciousness called soul with characteristic attributes and identity of all living organisms.

Much of the confusion has arisen in literature because various specialists indiscriminately use different terminologies for describing essentially the same thing. Thus, energy or frequency pattern mentioned by a physicist, a life force or information by a biophysicist, God by a religious preacher, or 'consciousness' and 'soul' by a metaphysicist or a quantum physicist, in fact, synonymously refers to the same common constituent of everything existing in the universe. Therefore, all that has gone into literature on the subject of consciousness needs to be rationalized or standardized with a uniform terminology of common human perceptions in general. When energy, consciousness/information, or life force slows down, it comes into being 'in formation', that is, coming into form and materialization. Water vapours condensing into liquid and further into solid crystalline ice by cooling exemplify such transformations. Similarly, the highly vibrating energy in the universe materializes according to some higher law or principle (still unknown). Plato, the Greek philosopher, suggested that at the most fundamental level, each element is made up of tiny components, each with the shape of a regular solid, assuming only five possible crystalline forms as described by Plato, namely, polyhedron, cube, dodecahedron, tetrahedron, and octahedron. For this reason, the regular solids are often known as the Platonic solids or Platonic crystals.

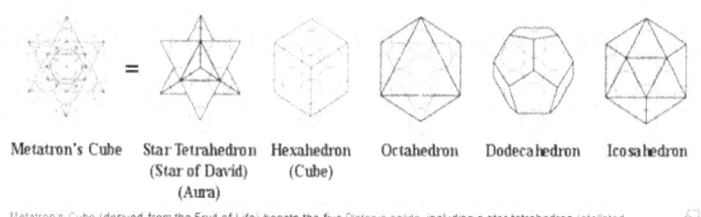

| Metatron's Cube | Star Tetrahedron (Star of David) (Aura) | Hexahedron (Cube) | Octahedron | Dodecahedron | Icosahedron |

Metatron's Cube (derived from the Fruit of Life) begets the five Platonic solids, including a star tetrahedron (stellated octahedron)

Platonic Crystal Structural Forms

According to Plato's scheme, earth is formed of cubes, fire is formed of tetrahedral, air is formed of octahedral, and water is formed of icosahedra. The motivation for this model seems to be the idea that the triangular faces of the tetrahedral, octahedral, and icosahedra could be rearranged like atomic units. This would enable the fundamental tetrahedral, octahedral, and icosahedra to transmute into one another, and thereby explain the alchemical transformation of matter from one kind into another. Plato considered the heavens to be eternal and unchanging. Celestial matter, in

Plato's view, was therefore composed of a single, perfect fifth element, and heavens according to him were associated with the fifth regular solid, the dodecahedron.

The geometric form of the crystal determines the content of condensed energy/life force/consciousness/ soul or information. This condensed energy is stored in the grid structure of the crystal known as 'crystal lattice' by the physicists. The term 'crystal' in fact means 'all consciousnesses'. No wonder, every kind of matter, both animate (proteins, nucleic acid, cellulose, sugars, carbohydrates) and inanimate (salts) in the universe are crystalline (conscious) in nature, as evidenced and elucidated by X-ray and electron diffraction techniques. Amorphous materials, beyond limits of detection by X-Ray or electron diffraction techniques, exhibit weird properties.

1.16 Mind as a Dynamic Responsive Attribute and Also a Reflection of the Body Interacting with Continually Changing Fluxes of Universal Energy

The earliest description of the individual 'self' expressed through mind and its identification with the 'universal soul' came from the Vedas and Upanishads which declared—*aham brahmasmi* (I am the universal conscious being). The driving force within the bodies of conscious organisms and that of in the universe outside was recognized to be the same. If this is so, then hydrogen protons and electrons and their flow as electric currents within the nerves, muscles, and across cell membranes of organisms comes to mind instantly, as they are universally all-pervading. Neurological symptoms such as loss of consciousness, confusion, forgetfulness, loss of memory, muscular dysfunction, partial or total paralysis of lower limbs, loss of hearing, blindness, and sleep disorders are all related and affected by the flow of electric currents. Dr Andrew Ure in 1818 demonstrated through his experiments on the cadaver body of an extremely muscular man, the sudden revival and commencement of breathing with application of an electric current to the phrenic nerve in the neck. The chest heaved and fell and the belly was protruded and collapsed. The touching of electrode from the battery to the supraorbital nerve induced the most extraordinary grimaces, such as 'rage, horror, anguish, dispair, sober, and ghastly smiles' on the face of the cadaver. Unfortunately, what we do not recognize is the fact that all living organisms are electrical machines and that electric currents lie at the heart of life itself. But this does not imply that electric charge or current itself is life, because electric charges emerge from a still deeper reality in the universe. There is a fundamental difference in the mode between the electricity that provides power to our bodies and that which lights our cities. While the electricity supplied to our homes is carried by the negatively charged subatomic particles called the electrons, almost all currents in the bodies of living organisms are carried by ions, electrically charged atoms. Of the five main ions that carry electric currents in our bodies, four are positively charged: sodium+, potassium+, calcium+, and hydrogen+ (protons) and, the fifth one, chloride is negatively charged. Movements of electrically charged ions constitute electric currents as nerve impulses that move into and across cell membranes. Electrical impulses travel along the length of our nerve and muscle fibres, and the ion currents that generate them flow at right angles to the direction of their travel. Another difference between electric current that lights our homes and the one that power our bodies is in the speeds of their transmission. Whereas an electric signal in a wire travels with the speed of light, that is, 186,000 miles per second, the electric nerve impulses travel at the speed of a mere 0.07 miles per second. The electrical impulses we generate for the beating of our hearts are only a few millionth of an ampere of current. We have come to understand the origin of bioelectricity and how the molecules (the ion channels) responsible for the electrical activity actually look like only since the last two decades. Human beings and all other life forms as part of the nature are being constantly bathed by the terrestrial and universal cosmic energy and our body epigenetically remains in perpetual dynamic interaction with this energy. These dynamic interactions are adjustments to the ever-fluctuating fluxes of universal energy, which create a constantly dynamic demand for secretion or synthesis of proteins, enzymes, coenzymes, or other metabolites in our body systems as a means and matter of survival strategies. The nature of secreted hormones, enzymes, and other metabolites together with proteins are responsible for our expressed thoughts, desires, moods, and other forms of emotional reactions which are generally characterized and attributed to our enigmatic mind. No wonder, since the energy fluxes are perpetually changing around us, so also our mind fluctuates as a part of dynamic adjustment of our body metabolism to shifting universal energy. These are subtle phenomena occurring at quantum or sub-quantum levels. However, we can easily feel, realize, experience, and understand them from our reaction, behaviour, and state of mind when we are exposed to sudden variations in ambient temperature, pressures, climatic and weather conditions, and other environmental fluctuations, and from the emotional demands generated in our body and mind under those conditions to comfort or ease ourselves.

Perhaps, modern science will never come to solve the mystery of the soul until and unless the nature and make-up of the most primordial energy from which all other forms of matter are formed is finally resolved. And yet, we find the most elaborate and profound descriptions about the constitutional make-up of the soul in the Vedas and Upanishads. These descriptions for over 8,000 years have not been scientifically proved or disproved, nor have been surpassed with a more profound concept, theory, or thought. The Vedic description about the structure and constitution of the soul still continues to rule and tries to satisfy human curiosity. T.D. Singh, in presenting the Vedantic model for the interaction of consciousness with matter, very rightly suggests that the present scientific research and inquiry should be expanded to include knowledge in search of spiritual truth. What is amazing is that the concepts and ideas about quantized nature of energy and universal existence was factually known to the saints and rishis in India almost 8,000 years before Christian era.

1.17 Vedic View of the Structure and Composition of Soul: The *Panchkosh Siddhanta*

It is clear from the discussions of this article that a very subtle, highly energetic, quantized form of universal energy is the undercurrent of all conscious life forms. This energy is mediated through ion channels as ionic electric currents within the bodies of all life forms to exhibit their conscious functions. The subtle form of this energy, possibly of the kind between pure magnetic (monopoles) and electromagnetic type, physical laws for its culmination and organization into a complex quantum called the soul for manifestation into conscious life forms, and the nature of its quantized behaviour are still not known to science, except the knowledge that the whole universe is electrical in nature and behaves as an electric entity. The rishis and saints belonging to the Vedic and Upanishad period in India (8,000 BC) not only pondered over the issue, but attempted to describe the structure and constitution of the soul on the basis of *Panchkosh Siddhanta* (five-shell model), an analogue of the modern concept of quantum packets of energy. The five shells of the soul, described in the Vedas, are:

(a) *Pranamaya Kosha* (lungs, breathing, and beating of the heart). Prana enters the body through the breath and is sent to every cell through the circulatory system.

(b) *Annamaya Kosha* (stomach, digestion of food, metabolism, and excretion)

(c) *Dnyanamaya Kosha* (mind, sensation, and experience)

(d) *Vidnyanamaya Kosha* (knowledge, analysis by brain, and perception), and

(e) *Anandamaya Kosha* (the connection and actual source of individual consciousness within the body and the universal source), perhaps merely represent the constituent parts of a variegated human body, which sustains, operates, and functions only because of the electrical current (electric charge) that flows through them.

The Panchkoshas do not factually represent the structural make-up of the individual soul, but the truth that operational functions of respiratory, digestive, excretory, and mental systems of all conscious organisms are functionally driven by the electric energy/electric charge and nothing else. For the sake of simplicity and explicit understanding of the human body mechanism, the prana energy/electrical atomic ionic movements has been classified into five kinds, depending on the functions they are used for, such as prana, *apan*, *udaan*, *saman*, and *vyan* that control our respiratory, excretory, vocal, digestive, muscular, and nervous systems respectively. The other ultimate form of prana called *dhananjaya* remains in atomic form even after death of the physical body. Intuitively, indeed this is nothing else but the electric charge that created, sustained, and drove the body as a conscious entity from birth to death and escapes to atmosphere. This is the only logical scientific explanation that connects well with modern scientific knowledge and the ancient Vedic concept. It is hoped that readers would appreciate and accept this explanation under the present state of knowledge.

According to the *Taittireeya Upanishad*, our physical body (and that of any living organism) is the *Annamaya Kosha*, that is, a shell/packet or body made up of food and juicy fluids. From a length of a mere one-and-a-half foot at birth, the Annamaya Kosha grows to about five or six feet with the accumulation of food and juicy fluids and with an increasing cell count and weight. Each and every cell of the body has a conscious soul (called *jeev*) in them. The 30 billion individual cells constituting a human body are coherently organized and put to multifunctional (involving the integrated work of eyes, nose, ears, and those of several organs) work in a cooperative way by the universal consciousness/energy/soul/prana or the electric charge. It is this prana that is believed to stay within Annamaya Kosha and drives each and every cell of the body as a whole. It dominates, rules, and governs all individual (jeev) souls of the cells and goads them to synthesize proteins, secrete enzymes, hormones, ATP molecules, and other forms of metabolites as demanded by the body, in its continual attempts to dynamically adjust itself to ever-changing flux of terrestrial and universal energies as a part of its survival strategy. These strategies include laughter, tears, thirst, hunger, rage, anger, love, happiness, satisfaction, physical movement of body, blissfulness, and a host of such other emotional states of experiences and responses. The proteins, enzymes, hormones, and other biochemicals, synthesized within our bodies under stimulation by the prana/universal energy/epigenetic or environmental conditions, generate an important and the most enigmatic attribute of the human being called the 'mind'. Since the intensity of the universal conscious energy flux changes every moment, the 'mind', which arises as an attribute from dynamic adjustments of body to universal flux of energy, also keeps continuously flickering. We thus see a deep logical connection and integration of the epigenetic principles with the terrestrial and universal environment in all living organisms as an integral part of nature. Mind as an attribute is also a kind of energy, and the location of its generation within mitochondria of each and every cell is also the *Pranamaya Kosha*. Since, according to modern physics, the entire energy in the universe is quantized, mind must also be quantized. Each and every kind of feeling, emotion, desire, lust, urge, etc. must be corresponding to differential energy packets of the 'mind quantum'. Mind also creates thoughts, but to create thoughts, there must be knowledge. *Taittireeya Upanishad* describes this knowledge as the inner body of the mind and intentionally calls it as the *Vidnyanamaya Kosha* to differentiate it from the universal knowledge *Dnyanamaya Kosha*. There are two categories of consciousness: universal and individual. The Supreme Being (prana) is conscious of everything in the universe, whereas the living entities (jeevas) are only conscious of themselves. The knowledge existing within the Vidnyanamaya Kosha of mind is only limited and restricted to the appropriate requirement of the biological species to which the body of the living organism (jeeva) belongs. All knowledge about the series of past reincarnations undergone by the living organism remains encoded and stored within this Vidnyanamaya Kosha. There is always a scope and freedom with the living organism to enlarge and enhance this knowledge and evolve itself into an organism of higher order within a pool of 8,400,000 kinds (combinations of genes) of possible living species in nature. And to help this evolution, the quantum of universal knowledge called the Dnyanamaya Kosha always lies within the core of the Vidnyanamaya Kosha. Quantized packets of knowledge, information, learning, memory of incidences, instances, trauma, sufferings of several past rebirths including those of the present birth etc. are encoded and stored within this Vidnyanamaya Kosha. The last of the quantum body is called the *Anandamaya Kosha*, wherein resides the primordial, omnipresent, omnipotent, conscious universal energy, supporting and holding all the outer quantum shells, such as the Vidnyanamaya, Manomaya, Pranamaya, and Annamaya Koshas. The crux of the riddle is—how these extremely energetic five quantum shells are sequentially connected to each other, and what is the nature of the force that binds them together for manifestation and exhibition in the form of a conscious, living human being. Perhaps, future developments in quantum chromodynamics (QCD), elucidating strong 'quark-quark' interactions (interactions between the ultimate forms of matter) may provide some explanation. The reference to 'sequential connection' mentioned earlier also suggests the presence of time, ingrained in the manifestation of the 'Panchkosha soul' as a living organism. As Halit Eroglu in his book, *The Theory of Everything*, emphatically suggests and innovatively interprets: 'When defining the time as the period between two events, then the time, or more specifically, a certain timing cycle, is the actual cause of the events. Without time, physical processes cannot take place, because there would be no "pulse" which could be addressed by the events. The events in the smallest dimensions do not take place themselves, while time is running alongside, but it is the quantized timing cycle which causes the events with its periodic sequences. All physical processes (therefore) depend on a universal timing cycle, whose sum we measure as an ordinary time, as Time Arrow, upon which the Cause–Effect principle is based. The time occurs in the smallest dimension and develops into bigger dimensions through the summation. Therefore our time interval of a "second" on a macroscopic scale is the sum of the quantized timing cycles in the Planck dimension. In the Planck sphere, there is plenty of time for the quantum events. The measured time is therefore dependent on the size of the scale. While on earth millions of years pass according to our time measurement, for an observer in the quantity of several million light years only some seconds would have elapsed according to his clock.'

Quite recently, Amit Goswami in his brilliant book, *Physics of the Soul: The Quantum Book of Living, Dying, Reincarnation and Immortality*, has attempted to describe the relationship between quantum physics and consciousness in describing the constitution of soul, which he calls a 'quantum monad', and readers are recommended to refer to this for comprehensive details.

In the end, I would just like to confess that I have not discovered or rediscovered the soul. I have merely attempted to reinterpret the ancient concept of the soul that we have been holding dear to our heart and carrying forward from one generation to the next in the light of modern science with the conviction that there had never been a thing as 'soul' in nature, as we are generally given to visualize. For thousands of years, our search for the soul has just been a chase for the proverbial 'wild goose' that factually does not exist. Electrical charge is the fundamental reality and it is electric charge that forms, sustains, and disintegrates material structures and drives the universe from stars, planets, and galaxies to inanimate and animate matter. Electric charge is the de facto soul, and it is this mighty force that recycles everything in this universe. The author will not be surprised if he has to revise the contents of the present book in a couple of years from now, in a more assertive way and in the light of the stormy discoveries, experimental evidences, and reinterpretations of the known phenomenon in view of the New Theory of Electric Universe and the Thunderbolt Project.[8] According to the Electric Universe Theory, black holes, dark matter, and dark energy do not exist; the Big Bang never happened; Einstein's theories of relativities are laughable fictions; electric currents that flow along plasma filaments shape and power galaxies; the currents stream into stars and power them like fluorescent bulbs; they induce the births of new planets; electric arcs create craters on the surfaces of planets; and electricity fundamentally explains all this stuff in a more comprehensive and logical way.

---

8 See for detailed information, Sarah Scoles, 'The People Who Believe Electricity Rules the Universe', (www.motherboard.vice.com/read/ electric-universe-theory-thunderbolts-project-wallace-thornhill).

Chapter 2
Questions about Soul and Rebirth:
Need for a Fresh Look and Redefinition

2.1 Abstract

The concepts of soul and rebirth have been connected with human life and psyche since the Vedic civilization (20,000 BC). Practically, every religion and civilization on the earth, irrespective of geographical location, nationality, levels of educational, scientific, and technological developments, have believed in the existence of soul and the concept of rebirth. However, tremendous developments in science (particularly physics and biology) and increase in level of instrumental detection and resolution limits, since the beginning of the twentieth century, have not only changed human life but have revolutionized our thoughts, concepts, perceptions, and views about the whole gamete of energy, matter, space, time, consciousness, and nature of reality in the universe. All these developments call for an entirely new approach to looking at all our traditional concepts and their interpretations, purely on the basis of science and scientific logic, developed since the beginning of the twentieth century. It has been argued that the activities of a conscious organism, generally attributed to the soul, are nothing but the result of the electric charges and the flow of electrically charged atomic ions and ionic currents across biomolecules and cellular membranes through millions of ion channels established within the developing and developed bodies of both unicellular and multicellular, multi-organ, living entities. Similarly, it has been logically argued that there is no possibility of any individual taking a rebirth after death. The whole concept of rebirth is linked to the memory of an individual who was born and lived in the past and which is perpetuated in the mind of the individual or in the social memory through historical records. In the absence of such a memory or record, the concept of rebirth of an individual from a historical past loses all its meaning, relevance, and significance.

Developments in modern physics suggest no such possibility for the rebirth of an individual after death. However, it provides ample scope, opportunity, and provision for the culmination of conditions, irrespective of time frames, locations, parentage, religious beliefs, nationalities, colour of skin, and sex of an individual, to be born with characteristics, properties, and traits of head, heart, and valour, similar to the one who had been born earlier in the historical past, and reminiscences about whom have been preserved in social memory and documented records. In this context, it has been argued that stories about Shri Krishna and Gautama Buddha remembering all of their past births and rebirths cannot be factually true. These stories have descended to us from third-person accounts. There is a possibility of a distortion or misinterpretation percolating down for centuries without rethinking, introspection, reasoning, or questioning. Therefore, these stories merely appear to be the metaphoric personal examples, cited on behalf of Shri Krishna and Gautama Buddha, for explaining the factual reality and law of perpetual creation, temporary subsistence, and destruction of all material (both inanimate and animate) going on in the universe. It has therefore been pleaded that when developments in science and technology are driving the twenty-first century, scientists must come forward to explain and reinterpret our traditional concepts purely on the basis of modern science, developed particularly after the beginning of twentieth century without any fear and free from personal, social, religious biases, and dogmatic belief.

It is now known that the entire universe constitutes nothing but an interplay of matter and energies of various kinds governed by four kinds of natural forces, namely weak interactions, strong interactions, electromagnetic, and gravitation. All material in the universe is made of atoms and the structures built from them. All atoms in the universe are available in only 118 different kinds and that too in very limited proportions and quantities. These atoms themselves are 'conscious entities', simply because of the fact that they all have retained their individual nature, properties, and characteristics besides their personal identities as to who they are, ever since they were first created in the nuclear furnaces of stars during the Big Bang explosion (that occurred about 14 billion years ago). The author believes that modern developments in the fields of molecular biology, epigenetic, biocentrism, chemical kinetics, morphogenetic field, stellar chemistry, string theory, and particle physics can be used in a multidisciplinary way to explain our traditional concepts on modern scientific logic. We cannot let our twenty-first century generation to remain scientifically unaware and ignorant and be the victims of outdated religious dogmatic belief and blind faith and continue to oppose new science. The author is hopeful that the readers would sincerely introspect and appreciate his exasperation and dilemma in comprehending the traditional concepts as are being described in innumerable books in a conventional way.

2.2 Introduction

Ever since the beginning of the ancient Vedic civilization and Vedic philosophy, which flourished in India almost 20,000 years BC, the concept of soul has remained attached to human life, psyche, and thought. This concept has also been upheld by other religious philosophies and civilizations that have followed and flourished on earth, irrespective of geographic locations, nationalities, scientific and technological developments, colour of inhabitants, and levels of education.

The singular oldest 'Vedic concept of soul' must have, probably and logically, spread globally by word of mouth through frequent travellers, merchants, and scholars who came to India from different lands and returned to their native countries, or by those preachers from India who either travelled on their own or were sent by the feudal kings to different realms for the purpose of spreading the message of the Vedas and Upanishads. Vedas are the oldest known philosophical texts in the world that form the tenets of the Sanatana Hindu way of living. Later in history, Emperor Ashok is reported to have deliberately sent teams of scholars and preachers to distant and neighbouring lands to spread Buddhist philosophy and ideology. No wonder, places connected to Buddha are still found in Afghanistan (west of India), China, Myanmar (Burma), and Japan in the east to Sri Lanka (Ceylon), Malaysia (Malaya), Thailand, Cambodia, and Indonesia in the south-east. In view of the missing links and documentary records on the visits and travels of each and every one of those who came to the Indian subcontinent, there is merit, logic, and also reason to believe that the concept of soul, in varying forms, shades, definitions, and ideas, might have also independently originated, evolved, or refined by civilizations in other places. Whatever may be the truth, the concept of soul has factually remained one of the most profound enigmatic mysteries to human beings to this day. The soul and its integration with religion, mind, and spirituality should have virtually driven millions of men and women from all parts of the world 'crazy' to search for it, discover it, feel or sense it, visualize, understand, realize, identify, explain, and even describe it as a common thread that binds all conscious living creatures together on earth and possibly in the universe. Today, all civilizations, religious groups, and philosophies in the world accept and regard the soul as something that drives the entire animate kingdom—from humans, animals, insects, fish, and plants to the unicellular organisms. Although some evidence has been claimed about the soul taking a rebirth and life after death, there is no unanimity over the concept and belief on rebirth of souls and their transmigration between and across species of all life forms for various reasons.

The soul, as a common constituent of all living entities, is considered and believed to be universal and indestructible. Surprisingly then, where is the question of its birth, death, and rebirth? The conscious mobility of living entities supposedly done at the instance of the 'soul' is in fact the attribute and handy work of electric charge and ionic currents, depending upon the nature and kind of atoms involved, which themselves are conscious entities. The bodies of living creatures constitute nothing more than a lump of ordinary matter, comprising of atoms of a few specific kinds, and the 'mind' appears to be an attribute arising out of the collective experience, feelings, and electrical activity of a thousand kinds of biomolecular proteins, synthesized within millions of individual cells of the body as a part of its coherent strategy for survival, in response to the continually changing environment. Therefore, each and every cell of the body, according to Candace B. Pert, constitutes the mind. Mind is regarded as the owner of experiences and feelings, the centre or focus of thoughts. According to David Hume[9]: 'The self is nothing but a collection of experiences: When I enter most intimately into what I call myself, I always stumble upon some particular perception or other, of heat or cold, light or shade, love or hatred, pain or pleasure. I can never catch myself at any time without a perception, and never can observe anything but only perception.'

2.3 A Case of Factual Reality and Redefining Rebirth

Extraordinary human individuals are immortalized by society in public memory because of their morals, thoughts, literary contribution, work, ideals, actions, valour, and compassion rather than for the size of their physical body,

9 David Hume, Chapter 6 in *A Treatise of Human Nature* 1(4), P.H. Nidditch (ed.) (Oxford University Press, 1978 [1739]).

appearance, and physique. Thousands of years after Shri Krishna mentioned about remembering his own innumerable births and rebirths in the *Gita*, it was Gautama Buddha who has been reported to have distinctly remembered all his past births and deaths, which include 357 lives as a human beings, 66 as gods, and 123 as animals, indicating thereby a possibility of transmigration from human to 'godly angelic' individuals to the animal life forms in-between successive births. Surprisingly however, there is neither the mention nor description of the sequential order of the births and rebirths of Gautama Buddha. In both these cases, it is impossible to believe that both Shri Krishna and Gautama Buddha should have factually remembered their individual identity through all the cycles of their births, deaths, and rebirths. It seems more probable, reasonable, logical, and scientifically consistent to believe that Shri Krishna and Gautama Buddha, being knowledgeable about Vedic philosophy and Upanishads, were in fact, citing their own lives, deaths, and rebirths as metaphoric examples in explaining the cardinal principle of perpetually cyclic nature of material creation, existence, and destruction going on in the universe. This cycle is common to both the inanimate and animate matter and nothing more. It is perhaps our enamoured love, affection, appreciation, and emotional attachment to the personalities, qualities, and teachings of both Shri Krishna and Gautama Buddha individually that have blinded us to overlook the factual scientific truth in their statements and mistakenly assume them to being endowed with supernatural powers. Both Shri Krishna and Gautama Buddha were humans, like any other individual. Shri Krishna was bestowed and invoked with godhood more than 2,500 years after his death, as per records mentioned by Dr P.V. Vartak, and Gautama Buddha, during his own lifetime, had clearly emphasized that he was neither a God nor a messenger of a God. His enlightenment was not the result of supernatural prowess, power, process, or agency, but rather the result of close and minute attention that he paid to the nature of the human mind which could be rediscovered by anyone for himself/ herself.

2.4 Possible Role of Synthesized Proteins in Controlling Behaviour, Actions, and the State of Enlightenment

Enlightenment is a process of being developed. It represents an emotional state of complete transformation from within, and develops from the inner depth of a focused mind with full force of concentrated urge. Obviously, this type of complete transformation can only be possible by controlling the induced synthesis of specific hormones, proteins, and glandular secretions through control of thoughts and concentration of the mind. It is well known that emotions and experiences are strongly influenced by physical effects, such as sound and the chemical composition of blood and hormonal imbalances. No wonder why the Vedas, Upanishads, and the *Gita* emphasize on controlling thoughts by way of practising meditation. It is now scientifically known, for sure, that our thoughts control the secretion of hormones and synthesis of proteins in the body, and the proteins manage and modify metabolic, muscular, and physiological behaviour that ultimately leads to physical actions and their reactions. Our five senses together form a single, integrated sensory system that is essentially designed to perceive a physical reality, and man creates his own reality through actions and thoughts. Therefore, enlightenment essentially means to learn how to control thoughts and focus the mind to regulate the secretion of hormones in order to balance the synthesis, nature, kind, and extent of specific proteins as a consequence. The state of mental and body condition experienced under the influence of such specifically induced and synthesized proteins by way of meditative practises may possibly be the experienced blissful state of what we call 'the enlightenment'. The very fact that a rigorous practical training is essential for controlling the mind for years (according to the 8 principles of performing yoga, that is, *Yama*, *Niyama*, *Asana*, *Pranayam*, *Pratyahara*, *Dharana*, *Dhyana*, and *Samadhi* stated by Patanjali in order to experience a blissful condition), probably indicates the factual truth of this phenomena and reality and its linkage to proteins. While Yama, Niyama, and Asana constitute the principle at the physical level, Pranayam and Pratyahara operate at the level of the mind and are essentially concerned with breathing exercises for regulation of mind and energy and managing the deviation of mind to the external world through the five senses. Truly speaking, the vocabulary for explaining the exact stage/state of what we call 'enlightenment' has not yet been born, but the role of synthesized proteins under the strict control of mind in meditation seems to be the most logical scientific possibility. The other attributes induced and expressed by human beings—as a consequence of the syntheses and secretion of specific hormones, enzymes, proteins, or other metabolites within the body initiated or ignited by particular thoughts, food, ailment, injury, inhalation, or excitement, etc.—are the expressions of kindness, love, affection, gratitude, sympathy, beauty, aesthetics, mood, art, music, anger, rage, hunger, sex, allergies, and such other subtle emotions.

2.5 Religious Philosophies Based on Third-Person Accounts

It is a historical fact that stories about the life, work, and philosophy of Shri Krishna and Gautama Buddha and also of Jesus Christ, Prophet Muhammad, and Lord Mahavira were written, compiled, and interpreted by their followers long after they were gone. Neither of them had told, nor even written their own biographies. Information about all of them has descended down to us from the records written by third persons, either contemporary or otherwise. The *Mahabharata* itself has seen three editions before coming into its present form, from originally containing 8,800 verses written by Ved Vyasa to 24,000 verses in the version edited by Rishi Vaishampayana and finally to 100,000 verses in the version compiled and edited by Rishi Sauti, sequentially, within a span of about one thousand years from Ved Vyasa[10]. Therefore, there appears to be something fundamentally wrong or, quite possibly, a distortion in communication and in understanding the messages of both Shri Krishna and Gautama Buddha about the factual reality or mystery of remembering their own births and rebirths. Even in the epic *Ramayana*, Shri Rama has been essentially described as an ordinary human being throughout the text except when a brief mention has been made of Rama as an incarnation of Vishnu in the 'Bal-Kaand' and 'Sunder-Kaand' chapters.

Innumerable instances have again been documented, at least in the cases of enlightened saints, prophets, rishis, and spiritually pious people, where they temporarily appeared in physical forms at different locations simultaneously to help or guide their disciples in difficulty. If such appearances are factually true, since he/she is carrying his/her personal traits and qualities with himself/herself, then why should these not be considered as the cases of simultaneous rebirths of the same individual because he or she is carrying all his personal traits and qualities with himself/herself to be justified as a rebirth? Forget, for the time being, the mode of such appearances or how this is possibly done and explainable on the basis of quantum physics. Against this argument, it is evident why identical twins or identical-looking father–son or mother–daughter combinations cannot be considered as rebirths or simultaneous rebirths because such individuals are entirely different in their personal characteristics, except in physical looks. Rebirth, in that event, needs to be redefined and not be restricted to being born only after his/her death in the previous life in a sequential order, irrespective of the irregular time gap between successive deaths and rebirths. Without consideration of the concept of 'free will', all natural processes are bound to be regularly cyclic and periodic.

10 The three editions of the *Mahabharata* by N.R. Waradpande (free download from www.nrwaradpande.in)

Incidentally, all stories about rebirths, therefore, appear to have possibly survived and prevailed for thousands of years under the dogmatic influence of religious thoughts and the continued belief in the existence of something unknown, the soul or superintelligence, at the back of our mind since childhood. No wonder, almost all scientific books, published till the end of the nineteenth century, invoked the element of God and His divine hand in one way or the other. Even the most revolutionary scientist of all times, Sir Isaac Newton, was not free from the dogmatic bondage with religious yoke. Tremendous developments in science and technology starting from the beginning of the twentieth century have completely revolutionized our perceptions and concepts about the nature, forms, manifestations, and interactions of energies, universe, material creation, and reality. Subjects such as soul, mind, consciousness, mind–matter interactions, telepathy, tele-transportation, clairvoyance, spirituality, etc., which have dominated human life and psyche for thousands of years, are no longer considered to be unscientific and exclusive domains of religion, religious preachers, and philosophies. They need to be integrated with physical sciences as a part and parcel of the continual interplay of universal energy–matter continuum and laws that govern their interactions. Soul, consciousness, mind, psyche, and such entities, in whichever form and energy, cannot be different, but must form a part and parcel of our universal creation. These subjects today are being profusely funded by government and private funding agencies for putting them on rational modern scientific logic and foundation. Acharya Rajneesh (Osho) was perhaps right when he said: 'Religions that do not evolve themselves in line with modern science and technology will have no option but to die'. It is therefore imperative on the part of global scientific community to look dispassionately at these subjects and at the traditionally inherited concepts of thousands of years from a purely scientific point of view, and justifiably interpret them more as problems of multidisciplinary and interdisciplinary continuum of modern scientific knowledge developed only after the beginning of the twentieth century. If religious leaders do not volunteer and take initiative to integrate religion with modern science, the scientific community must take such an initiative in explaining the illusive religious/ metaphysical concepts on scientific theories. It cannot be denied that science also has something to say about religious matters. Topics such as the nature of time and space, the origin and nature of matter and life, or causality, free will, and determinism, etc., the very conceptual framework in which the religious questions have been posed, can be altered by scientific advances. Some of the theological issues of the past centuries have been rendered meaningless by modern cosmology and science. Even Albert Einstein admitted: 'We believe that science serves humanity best when it is all free of influence by any dogma and reserves the right to question all assumptions, including their own', and, 'It is more difficult to break a prejudice than an atom.'

2.6 Our Criteria for Considering and Accepting Rebirth

The only justified measure/criteria, so far, for our consideration in accepting rebirth has been the accidental birth of an individual born in an entirely different timescale and location, under an entirely different combination of genetic, epigenetic, environmental, terrestrial, and celestial configurations, conditions and circumstances, resembling exactly or near-exactly in similarities and characteristics of personality, traits, and quality of certain exalted thoughts, ideals, sagacity, behaviour, action, and leadership with any person, who had been born in the historical past, and memories about whom are perpetually ingrained in our social memory or in documentary records. In the absence of such a memory or documented history, the question of rebirth loses all significance and relevance. The physical body, appearance, characteristics, parentage, geographic location, nationality, religious faiths or year, and time of birth, practically, are given no consideration, except exact or near-exact correspondence of the qualities of head, heart, and thoughts in deciding a rebirth of an individual from the past. It is again a practical social truth that any individual born with corresponding characteristics of the personality and brilliance of Shri Krishna or Gautama Buddha will reform the society around him. The uncertainty principle enunciated by Werner Heisenberg states that no two events are exactly alike and that the statistical probability for such incidences to coincide may be one in a billion. That leaves no scope for a possible rebirth of an individual after his/her death, but, at the same time, suggests the possibility for an individual to be born in future with the qualities of head, heart, and mind similar or nearly similar to anyone who had previously lived on the earth, since the entire universe contributes to what we are. Perhaps, the meaning of the well-cited and very often repeated couplet from the *Gita—Yada yada hee dharmasya, glaneer bhavati Bharat, Abhyuthanam adharmsya tadatmaanum srujamyaham; Paritranaya sadhunam, vinashaya cha dushkrutam, Dharmasanstha panarthay, Sambhavaamee yugey yugey* (O Bharata, whenever there is deterioration of dharma, leading to chaos and rise of *adharma*, I embody Myself to halt deterioration and put evolution on proper track; for the protection of the righteous and the destruction of the wicked, as well as for the strengthening of the foundation of dharma, I am born time and again)[11]—essentially conveys this scientific message and nothing more.

The belief in rebirth is attempted to be justified by advancing an argument that the living soul of the creature carries memory of its actions, learning, and characteristics to its new birth after death. There is no unanimity over how exactly this is possible, on the nature and structure of 'soul', and on the nature and kind of forces or energy that are involved in the transfer of memory from one soul in one life

11 Chapter 4, *Gita*, verses 7, 8, reference 14, pp. 112–13

to that in the next. This justification, instead of satisfactorily answering the problem, has raised new questions on the exact location of memory in the body; how, where, and which organ is involved; in what form they are recorded, stored, and recalled; the nature and form of the vehicle and mode of transferring memory during cycles of birth, death, and rebirth. Here, even if we assume for the time being that the soul itself carries its memories from one life to the other as the vehicle of transfer, the *Garbha Upanishad*, on the contrary, clearly states that a foetus growing in the womb of its mother becomes jeeva (conscious self) in the seventh month and becomes complete in every sense to be a person in the eighth month. Clearly, in the seventh month of the growing stage of the foetus, the developing ion channels in its body become fully operational to exchange ions and conduct ionic currents, that is, it is the stage at which the ionic electric currents begin flowing and consciousness (as electrical activity) appears, or, analogically, the soul enters the foetus. The fully developed foetus, as a person, by the end of the eighth month is believed to forget all memories of its past lives, births, deaths, and acts before its birth. Here again, there is an unjustified assumption that the foetus had carried its memories from the past until then, when it itself comes to conscious state in the eighth month. The *Sarvasa Upanishad* however mentions that a subtle body (linga deha) is created as an attribute from the mind and other subtle elements that reside in the knot of the heart, and the consciousness within this body is the 'knower of the field'. What is this subtle element that resides in the knot of the heart? Has it got something to do with the power grid of consciousness, the *anahata chakra* or the heart chakra, which creates the field of coherence around the body? Obviously, the answers to these questions are not easy, but in attempts to justify and support the devised line of thinking, theories on transmigration of memory from one life to another were invented, developed, and invoked. The theory of karma from the Vedic times to the theory of morphogenetic fields and morphic resonance by Rupert Sheldrake in recent years are the most popular examples. However, both these theories, representing bold attempts for explaining rebirth and the mode of transfer of memory from one life to the other, fundamentally presuppose the existence of the soul to be a factual reality of animate and inanimate material creation in nature. Perhaps, the memory of our dogmatic socio-religious thought, perpetuated in our personal, community, and social life system for thousands of years about the existence of some superintelligence, is preventing us from taking an objective, fresh look, purely from the scientific point of view.

2.7 Everything in the Universe Is Made of Atoms

It is now known that our physical existence is nothing more than an ordinary part of the cyclic creation of animate and inanimate matter in nature under the control of only four kinds of natural forces—weak interactions, strong interactions, electromagnetic, and gravitation. Everything in the animate and inanimate material world is made of atoms, and it is the kind, nature, proportion, condition, environment, and configuration of their combinations that determine the physical form, chemical properties, traits, and behaviour of all kinds of the structures formed. We have learned that the living and lifeless matter do not differ in any fundamental way. There is no definite stage of complexity at which life appears, and there is no definite stage of evolution in which the mind develops in living organisms. Therefore, consciousness and memory appear to be ingrained in the atoms and in their structures themselves. The 118 different kinds of atoms, available in limited quantities in nature today, were created at the time when the Big Bang occurred. All these atoms have retained their identities (and, of course, the memory of who they are) ever since then. It is pertinent to ask if our own memory is a culmination of the combined probability attributes of the individual memories of all atoms that constitute our body, or that of the soul, if it factually exists, or, more particularly, of the varying nature, kind, and the amount of thousands of proteins synthesized within our body system. Perhaps, the last possibility appears to be scientifically more realistic than others because proteins in living organisms have a flexible structure, very little thermal disorder at room temperatures and, despite not being liquids, they move freely and exhibit the properties of consciousness. Our soul has also been logically and analytically described to be an attribute of ionic currents and electrical activity of all the atoms that constitute our body and it is likely that we have failed to recognize electric charge (hydrogen, proton, and electron, its negative equivalents, to be the de facto soul that drives all conscious creatures). If this is so, then it could be explained that why an individual with Alzheimer's disease loses his memory and identity on the basis of the nature, kind, and the amount of new proteins synthesized in his body after contracting the ailment. We cannot predict when a man will die, but we can certainly predict how many men in a country or from a community belonging to different age groups will die in a year on the basis of modern quantum physical methods.

Joel Steinheimer, a renowned quantum physicist and mathematician, in his remarkable studies on epigenetic regulation of biosynthesis of proteins in plants, translates composed, audible musical vibrations into corresponding quantum vibrations that occur at the molecular level, as a protein gets assembled in a plant from its constituent amino acids. By using simple physics, Steinheimer[12] composes musical notes that achieve this correlation. Each musical note which he composes for the plant is a multiple of original quantum frequencies that occur when the quantum-particulate molecules of amino acids join to assemble the protein chain. Playing the right kind of musical tune stimulates the formation of a plant's protein and increases its growth. The length of a note corresponds to the real time it

12 Joel Steinheimer, http://www.earthpulse.com /science/songs.html.

takes for each amino acid to join next during the assembly of protein molecular structure. Steinheimer's research clearly shows that the characteristics and experiences of a plant are determined by the external epigenetic environment and by the nature and kind of induced synthesized proteins by the stimulus from external (and also internal) environment during growth.

2.8 Need for a New Thinking and Explanation on Our Traditional Concepts

Even if we assume that some form of soul persists beyond death, it remains to be explained what particles of material or non-material stuff that soul is made of. What kind and nature of known or unknown forces hold it to the animate life forms, and how does it interact with ordinary matter? Unfortunately, no advocates of the existence of souls, their transmigration, and life after death, has tried to sit down and do the hard work of explaining how the basic physics of atoms that constitute the entire universal animate and inanimate material creations, consisting of electrons, protons, and neutrons, laid down by the standard model of particle physics and quantum physics would have to be altered, used, or interpreted in order for this to be true. Humanity has so far remained divided on this account for various reasons, which have been effectively summarized by Moharir in his comprehensive multidisciplinary review on the subject. Stories about rebirth of souls and their transmigration are enjoying credence and circulation in all languages, communities, societies, and nationalities, irrespective of the nature and form of political systems and levels of scientific and technological developments. Moharir, in this holistic article, has attempted to describe the concept of soul on the basis of modern scientific logic and has pleaded for evolving a universal consensus opinion for rationalization and standardization of various terminologies, free from socio-religious fears, personal biases, prejudices, preferences, and dogmas, being indiscriminately used by people from different disciplines in essentially describing the same thing. As a consequence, the energy or frequency pattern mentioned by a physicist, or a life force or information by a biophysicist, or God by a religious preacher, 'consciousness' and 'soul' by a metaphysicist or a quantum physicist, in fact, synonymously refer to the same common constituent of everything existing in the universe. The confusion prevalent with respect to the inconsistent conflicting ideas and concepts in this area of research needs to be removed. Literature, on the subject of soul, written with limited, narrow, traditionally philosophical, psychological, religious, cultural, emotional, and dogmatically personal biases have complicated and confused the situation more than it has resolved for greater clarity, despite tremendous advancements in science, technology, and limits of instrumental resolution. Rarely has anyone described (or at least attempted to describe) the subject of soul from a holistic multidisciplinary perspective. No wonder, our understanding about the soul and mind continue to be mysteriously enigmatic, confusing, and dogmatically bound to the traditional yoke. It is high time to, at least, attempt to resolve the matter for good and set all speculations, fallacies, fictions, and subjective imaginations to rest, purely and almost exclusively on the strength of scientific logic and truth. This is particularly important in view of the fact that research on subjects like soul, mind, consciousness, mind–matter interactions, clairvoyance, spirits and spirit world, etc. are receiving increasing research funding on a global scale. Moreover, in the twenty-first century, when developments in scientific and technological areas are driving the civilization, we cannot allow humanity to be a persistent victim of ignorance, illiteracy, superstitions, blind faith, and confusion and continue to bear the burden of dogmatic religious views any more. It is the moral duty and responsibility of the global scientific community and the scientific academies, in particular, to rise above the narrow consideration of dogmas of various shades of opinions and educate the common man on the basis of scientific facts. Therefore, all that has gone into literature on the subject of soul needs to be rationalized on standardized uniform terminology of common human perceptions in general. There is, therefore, no reason, excuse, or justification on the part of any of our religious leaders to remain irresponsibly ignorant, aloof, isolated, or blinded from the developments in modern science and to keep their followers scientifically unaware, ignorant, illiterate, and brainwashed to remain dogmatically opposed to new scientific thinking. They first need to open up themselves, develop capacity to understand the new science, evolve with changing times, accept reality, and help in providing a scientific basis to their faiths before preaching to newer generations, because the only purpose of religions is to collectively and individually educate their followers to live mentally, thoughtfully, intellectually, knowledgably, academically, physiologically, nutritionally, and physically in sound health and in harmony with the laws of nature. It is therefore heartening, in contrast to the known history and traditionally orthodox and dogmatic attitude of the Vatican Church, that Pope Francis has recently, in 2014, endorsed the scientific theories of evolution and Big Bang to be factual realities. How I wish that the Islamic religious leaders from all nationalities would also take a step in this direction and help their followers in liberating themselves from outdated dogmatic yokes.

Keeping in correspondence with the developments in modern science and technology, the ancient Vedic and Upanishad philosophies (20,000 BC) from India, surprisingly, stand tall and scientifically relevant to a large extent even today. But, unfortunately, the scholars here are not even educating and explaining the fundamental science described in the Vedas, Upanishads, and the *Gita* to the common men. They merely retell stories and perform the ritualistic practises, traditions, and superstitions without reason, question, or independent thinking. The perfectly scientific treatises, such as the Vedas and Upanishads, continue to be erroneously described under Hindu religious literature. Unfortunately, Sanskrit language scholars from India rarely understand modern science, and scientists or physicists, on their part, neither learn nor understand Sanskrit. No wonder, therefore, why, ignorance, misconceptions, misunderstandings, confusions, and even incorrect interpretations of Vedic teachings continue to prevail amongst the larger section of masses. The author, without any reservation, heeds of what others might think of him and has no hesitation in admitting that with all intellectual honesty, his own attempts to sincerely understand the concepts of soul, consciousness, mind, and rebirth, etc. literally made his head hurt. Even reading the best of the scholarly books available, written by celebrated authorities from various segments of religious and philosophical schools without bias, malice, prejudice, doubts, or intentions of questioning their sincerity, honesty, convictions, and authority in attempting to write down their own thoughts in these books, have personally not been able to provide him (the author) clear mental images or comprehension about these concepts. Perhaps, the author himself lacks the kind of necessary sophistication to fully conceive all that is described in these books, when millions of other readers have rocked their heads, tamely accepted, and surrendered to their contents. They all have appeared to the author, a myriad collection of beautifully worded, strongly motivating, emotionally charged, masterly skilled, psychologically captivating, and mentally paralyzing and, yet, profound literary compositions of the choicest words and phrases, subjectively presenting individual perceptions, but still demanding clarity on the basis of modern scientific theories. The present article is therefore an outcome and reflection of the frustration of the author in trying to understand these concepts, which have been boggling human mind since time immemorial. I hope my readers would appreciate my sincere urge, hopeless frustration, and dilemma in my pursuit and convictions. Perhaps, they may patiently introspect and possibly identify themselves with me and justify the arguments raised in this article. They may even find themselves in no better situation than I am. Optimistically, a ray of hope may be seen in someone from somewhere on the horizon provoked from such an introspection.

The author is also of the sincere conviction that a holistic, plausible explanation for the soul, consciousness, mind, memory, and rebirth can be sought within the framework of multidisciplinary and interdisciplinary approach involving tenets of new theories on epigenetics, biocentrism, morphogenesis, morphic resonance, chemical reaction kinetics, stellar chemistry, quantum physics, quantum chromodynamics, string theory, the standard model of atomic structure, and molecular biology. We have perhaps not listened carefully to what nature has been trying to convey through the modern developments in physics without some kind of dogmatic bias at the back of our minds that all matter (atoms) has a rudimentary degree of consciousness, and that man and all animate life forms are a direct result of this property of matter or that of various kinds of field attributes generated by matter under specific constitution and configurations. Quantum mechanics, to that extent, is a mathematical description of the consciousness of matter.

2.9 References

1. Osho-Rajnish. 2015. 'Gita Darshan' 1 (8). Vidyut Kanon se Nirmeet Shareer. Osho World.

2. Schrodinger, Erwin. 1955. *What is Life?*. Cambridge: Cambridge University Press.

3. Lipton, Bruce H. 2005. The Biology of Belief: Unleashing the Power of Consciousness, Matter and Miracles. USA: Hay House, p. 202.

4. Lanza, Robert. 2013. 'A New Theory of the Universe'. *The American Scholar*.

5. Lanza, Robert and Bob Berman. 2009. *Biocentrism: How Life and Consciousness are the Keys to Understanding the True Nature of the Universe*. Dallas, TX: Benbella Books.

6. Ashcroft, Frances. 2012. *The Spark of Life: Electricity in the Human Body*. London: Penguin Books.

7. Pagels, Heinz R. 1982. *The Cosmic Code: Quantum Physics as the Language of Nature*. New York: Bantam Books.

8. Ho, Mae-Wan. 2008. *The Rainbow and the Worm: The Physics of Organisms*. Singapore: World Scientific, p.380.

9. Hey, Tony and Patrick Walters. 2003. *The New Quantum Universe*. Cambridge: Cambridge University Press, pp. 268–83.

10. Goswami, Amit. 2001. *Physics of the Soul: The Quantum Book of Living, Dying, Reincarnation, and Immortality*. Charlottesville: Hampton Roads Publishing Company, p. 288.

11. Cochran, A.A. 1971. 'Relationships between quantum physics and biology'. *Foundations of Physics*, 1(3): 235–50.

12. Guney, M.R. 2005. *Geetartha Vishwa*. Pune: Snehal Prakashan, pp 112–13.

13. Moharir, A.V. 2014. 'A Scientific Look at the Concept of Soul: An Attempted Synthesis'. *University News*, 52(29): 19–30. Also presented at the 88th Session of Indian Philosophical Congress, SV University, Andhra Pradesh, 17–19 October 2014.

14. Osborn, David H. (ed.). 2009–2010. *Science of the Sacred*. LuLu.com Publishers (pdf copy available online).

15. Osho. 2014. 'Dhyan Yog-Mool Sandesh'in Mana Hee Pooja, Mana Hee Dhoop (December), pp 16–18.

16. Pert, Candace B. 1997. Molecules of Emotion: Why You Feel the Way You Feel. London: Pocket Books.

17. Ross, Elisabeth Kubler. 2008. On Life After Death. USA: Celestial Arts.

18. Ross, Elizabeth Kubler. 1998. *The Wheel of Life: A Memoir of Living and Dying*. New York: Simon & Schuster, p.286.

19. Sheldrake, Rupert. 1995. A New Science of Life: The Hypothesis of Morphic Resonance. Rochester: Park Street Press.

20. Sheldrake, Rupert. 2011. Dogs That Know When Their Owners are Coming Home: And Other Unexplained Powers of Animals. New York: Three River Press.

21. Sheldrake, Rupert. 2011. The Presence of the Past: Morphic Resonance and the Habits of Nature. London: Icon Books.

22. Sheldrake, Rupert. 2012. The Science Delusion: Freeing the Spirit of Enquiry. Coronet.

23. Thakkar, Hirabhai. 2001. Theory of Karma. Ahmedabad: Kusum Prakashan.

24. Vartak, P.V. 1999. *The Scientific Dating of The Ramayana & The Vedas*. Pune: Ved Vidnyan Mandala, Vartak Ashram.

25. Vartak, P.V. 2011. *Yugapurush Shri Krishna* (2nd edn) Pune: Vartak Prakashan, Vartakashram.

26. Vartak, P.V. 2012. Punarjanma (6th edn). Pune: Shobhna Vartak Prakashan.

27. Vartak, P.V. 2012. *Upanishadanchey Vidnyan-Nishtha Nirupan* (VOL. 1, 6th edn). Pune: Vartak Ashram.

28. Vartak, P.V. 2013. *Upanishadanchey Vidnyan-Nishtha Nirupan* (VOL. 2, 6th edn). Pune: Vartak Ashram.

29. Weaver, Richard F. 2008. *We Are Our Ancestors*. Pennsylvania: RoseDog Books, p 156.

30. Weiss, Brian. 1988. Many Lives, Many Masters: The True Story of a Prominent Psychiatrist, His Young Patient, and the Past-Life Therapy That Changed Both Their Lives. New York: Simon & Schuster.

31. Zukav, Gary. 1989. *The Seat of the Soul*. London: Random House Books.

'The most merciful thing in the world ... is the inability of the human mind to correlate all its contents ... The sciences, each straining in its own direction, have hitherto harmed us little; but someday the piecing together of dissociated knowledge will open up such terrifying vistas of reality ... That we shall either go mad from the revelation or flee from the deadly light into the peace and safety of a new dark age.'

—H. P. Lovecraft

This paper was presented at the National Conference on Ancient Science and Technology, Retrospection and Aspirations (ASTRA 2015) Fergusson College, University of Pune, 10–11 January 2015. Proceedings of the Conference, ISSN. Academy of Sanskrit Research.

Biography of Prof Dr Ravin Lakshman Thatte (Ravin Thatte), MS, FRCS, Plastic and Reconstructive Surgeon, Mumbai, Maharashtra, India

International Honours

1. Fellowship of the Royal College of Surgeons, Edinburgh, ad hominem, for his scientific and social work (at that time, the first Asian to have received this fellowship).

2. Honorary membership of the British Association of Plastic Surgeons for his contribution to the science of plastic surgery.

3. Honorary membership of the Malaysian Association of Plastic Surgeons for his simple, yet, effective new techniques suitable for the developing world.

4. Fulbright Scholarship for advances for further research in venous flat circulation, a concept described by him. The research was carried out at the University of Alabama School of Medicine.

5. Recognized for five consecutive years in international yearbooks of plastic surgery for new original techniques.

6. Contributed chapters by invitation to the Encyclopaedia of Flaps.

7. Currently the author-compiler of a blog called 'shortnotesinplasticsurgery.wordpress.com', which has attracted a worldwide viewership of more than 200,000 (a project assigned to him by the Association of Plastic Surgeons of India).

8. Honoured by the Association of Plastic Surgeons of India as the 'Plastic Surgeon of the Year 2015' for his scientific contribution, social initiatives, and his work on spirituality.

9. Visiting lecturer in India and the world over in various teaching centres including Massachusetts General Hospital (Harvard University) and Royal Institute of Orthopaedics.
10. Awarded the Eponymous Graham Lecture of the Royal College of Surgeons, Edinburgh.

National Honours
1. Hari Om Ashram Rangachary Award of the Association of Surgeons of India.
2. Sangham Lal Award and Oration of the Academy of Medical Sciences, New Delhi, India.
3. Eric Peet Prize and Lecture of the Association of Plastic Surgeons of India.
4. Sushruta Prize and Lecture of the Association of Plastic Surgeons of India.
5. Lifetime Achievement Award of the Association of Plastic Surgeons of India.
6. M.V. Sant Award and Lecture of the B.Y.L. Nair Charitable Hospital, Mumbai, India.

Social Work in Medical Field
1. Established plastic surgical services at a rural hospital in Dervan, Ratnagiri, Maharashtra, India.
2. Director of Smile Train Project at the Godrej Hospital in Mumbai.
3. Founder-Trustee of the Swacchatanyas, a trust to improve the hospital conditions in Mumbai.

Other Environmental Work
1. In one of the first environmental battles in Mumbai, India, he created a large park with skating rink on a piece of land reserved for that purpose, but which was being unnotified for other purposes at the behest of a multinational conglomerate.
2. Cleaned up a beach and maintained it with a neighbourhood association in the suburb of Mahim in Mumbai.

3. As the secretary of his housing society, he won a municipal award for achieving zero-garbage through recycling and composting waste.

Work in Literature and Philosophy

1. A keen student of both Western and Indian philosophy. He has, in particular, studied *Dnyaneshwari*, a critical analysis of the *Bhagwadgita*, the most well-known treatise on Indian Philosophy. *Dnyaneshwari* is a 700-year-old narration in Prakrit, a predecessor of the modern Marathi language in India. The *Gita* has seven hundred verses and *Dnyaneshwari* has 9,000 verses. His analysis has a special emphasis on the scientific and rational basis of Indian philosophy, and he has written 8 books on the subject, one of which has won a state award for its philosophical and scientific outlook. He has also translated the *Dnyaneshwari* in English, which took him 6 years to compile. This book is now running into its fourth edition.

2. Written a historical travelogue of a part of the Western coast of India and its influence on Modern Indian History.

3. He has written a daily column and a weekly column on a variety of issues in two Marathi Language newspapers (*The Loksatta* and *The Maharashtra Times*), and one of those daily columns has now been published as a book.

Biography and Summary Statement on the Contribution of Dr. A.V. Moharir to Science

Anil Vishnu Moharir (b. 1944 at Nagpur), holds a masters degree in Physics from the Jiwaji University, Gwalior and PhD from the Indian Institute of Technology, Delhi. Starting his research career from the National Physical Laboratory in 1967, he joined IARI-ICAR service in 1968 and served in various capacities as senior research assistant, scientist, professor and head, Division of Agricultural Physics. He initially worked on spectroscopic, spectrophotometric, and electron microscopic studies of soils, plants, and other biological materials and developed accurate spectrophotometric methods for trace determination of iron and titanium, several techniques for practical transmission of electron microscopy, and a new technique of contact electron micrography for characterization of paper and thin film materials. Based on his studies on moisture hysteresis of seeds, he developed a simple laboratory procedure for screening drought-tolerant wheat and rice varieties for cultivation under rain-fed conditions and introduced a new concept of normalized moisture hysteresis, which has found practical use in bakery and biscuit industry. Later, he extensively studied the fine structure and structure–property relationships in native cotton fibres of varieties of all the four commercially cultivated species for helping cotton breeders in selecting parent genotypes for evolving new strains with inherent high fibre tenacity, as demanded by the modern Open-End-Rotor Spinning (OES) technology. From X-Ray diffraction studies on bundles of cotton fibres, he identified cellulose crystallite orientation index (Hermans Crystallite Orientation Factor) to be the best index for characterization of cotton for tensile strength, both within individual species, within mixtures of *diploid* and *tetraploid* species, and within a mixture of all species of cotton taken together. Prof Moharir has published over one hundred and twenty research papers in national and international journals, presented several papers at international conferences held in India, Germany, Belgium, and USA, invited as a keynote speaker, translated and edited books, poems, religious discourses, and texts from Hindi and Marathi into English. He served as honorary editor of the Indian Journal of Fibre and Textile Research (CSIR), Journal of Agricultural Research, editor-in-chief of the Journal of Agricultural Physics, as a regular referee for several other scientific journals, and as a panel scientist for the e-text book project of the National Institute of Science Communication (NISCOM-CSIR). A recipient of prestigious fellowships from the International Atomic Energy Agency, Vienna–Austria, and the Commission of the European Communities, Brussels–Belgium, Prof Moharir has successfully handled two international collaborative research projects on cotton. He has travelled extensively in England, Europe, Russia (USSR), and USA. Over half a dozen international biographical compilations on people of significant achievements have listed him for his contribution to science. Deeply interested in Hindustani classical vocal and instrumental music, Prof Moharir is himself an accomplished portrait artist in charcoal medium and a connoisseur of fine art. After retirement from service in 2006, he is actively working for Mission Health and Green India, besides regularly involved in freelance writing on various scientific subjects from multidisciplinary angles. His recent book *Profile in Solitude Felicitation of Professor Atmaram Bhairav (A.B.) Joshi on His Ninety-First Birthday with Foreword from Professor M. S. Swaminathan, Padma Vibhushan, FRS, FNI, FNAAS* is a de-facto national document on the life and contribution of Dr A.B. Joshi, the greatest agricultural scientist to India's first green revolution. His other books, *A Life of a Physicist in Agricultural Research* and *Random*

Walks in Solitude-Essays in Multidisciplinary Explorations in Science, have been extolled as the unique and scholarly contributions to science by Padma Bhushan Prof Ram Badan Singh, President National Academy of Agricultural Sciences, and by Prof Dr Yeshwant L. Nene, Chairman, Asian Agri-History Foundation. Professor Moharir served as a member of the National Panel of Eminent Citizens of the Ministry of Rural Development, Government of India, for evaluation of the projects executed under the Mahatma Gandhi National Rural Employment Guarantee Scheme (MGNREGA) in the state of Nagaland for over 2 years.

Other published books from the author;

1. *ME MY OWN*, English translation of *Mee Maaza* book of short poems in Marathi by Chandrashekhar Gokhale.

2. *Four Decades of Research in Agricultural Physics* (ed.), published by the Indian Agricultural Research Institute, New Delhi.

3. *Profile in Solitude: Felicitation of Professor Atmaram Bhairav Joshi on his Ninety-First Birthday* with Foreword by Padma Vibhushan Prof M S Swaminathan, FRS, FNI, FNAAS (ed.).

4. *A Life of a Physicist in Agricultural Research* with Foreword by Padma Bhushan Prof Ram Badan Singh.

5. *Random Walks in Solitude: Essays in Multidisciplinary Explorations in Science* with Foreword by Dr Yashwant L. Nene.